MULTIPLE PERSONALITIES

TATYANA SHCHERBINA

MULTIPLE PERSONALITIES

by Tatyana Shcherbina

Tatyana Shcherbina "Razmnozhenie lichnosti"
© 2010, Novoe Literaturnoe Orozrenie

Translated by Melanie Moore

Book created by Max Mendor

© 2015, Glagoslav Publications, United Kingdom
Glagoslav Publications Ltd
88-90 Hatton Garden
EC1N 8PN London
United Kingdom

www.glagoslav.com

ISBN: 978-1-78437-934-6

A catalogue record for this book is available
from the British Library.

CONTENTS

CHAPTER 1: PUSHKIN

I've got this persistent fantasy. It's Pushkin just before his wedding at the church at Nikitskiye Vorota, right near my house. He suddenly appears at the very same spot only it's 2006. Everyone, his young bride included, has vanished without trace and there he is standing on the pavement in his tails, gazing all around distractedly when who should come along but me. Unlike the other passers-by who think he's a street performer, one of those European-style living statues, an actor from the theatre on Malaya Bronnaya with a sudden urge to light a candle in the church, or a visiting musician looking for the Conservatory, I realize straight away that he's Alexander Sergeyevich Pushkin. And the reason I do is because, basically, I believe in time travel. If time travel didn't exist, clairvoyance would be impossible and clairvoyance does exist – I've tested it myself. Well, not tested it exactly but I have read many times of even uneducated children and adults coming round from an injury, starting to speaking in languages they don't know, and claiming to be other people. Tests have shown that at some time in the past those people really did exist. It's what's always used to prove that reincarnation is real as well. Whether what's happening is the transmigration of souls or the brief encounter of two non-contemporaries in a single body isn't known for certain. The injured recover and forget about their weird new incarnation as they go about their ordinary lives. Contact with past lives is rare but it does happen. Which means that time travel is theoretically possible.

Ah, yes, the fantasy.

"Alexander Sergeyevich, hello!" I say.

He looks at me, reluctantly tearing his eyes away from the church, and asks what's happened.

"Now, please don't get excited," I say in the wheedling tones of a psychiatrist because I can tell he's right on the verge of going mad. If he looks at the traffic jam on Bolshaya Nikitskaya for another five minutes, he'll lose all reason. I mean he has no clue there could ever be steel horses snorting not steam from their nostrils but exhaust fumes from their backsides. They don't even look like horses.

"Those are self-propelled carts," I say, taking his arm.

"What sort of carts?" he asks.

He snatches his arm away and, screwing up his face, looks me over from top to toe (taking in my haircut, jeans, polo-neck).

"My dear young lady, you must be with the circus."

I introduce myself quickly so as to move on to further explanations.

As luck would have it, Nikitskaya is one of the few streets in Moscow to have kept its old houses. Are they are old as Pushkin though? If it weren't for three grim-looking thirteen-storey tower blocks, the street could surely pass as authentic. Pushkin might not be able to tell the difference between mock nineteenth century buildings and his original surroundings. I attempt to divert the gaze of the poet, author, playwright, and lothario, who is at the same time both 30 and 200 years old (and the rest!) and at present has the air of a demented, woebegone midget, and distract him from the three Brezhnev-era towers, one of which happens to be where I live. If he would just look at the other side of the street which, in theory, shouldn't cause him any culture shock. I nudge him towards my own block because, if we take a dozen steps towards Nikitskiye Vorota he'll find a diminutive statue of himself and his wife under a small golden dome, and I'll be embarrassed. Right here and now I am the only person who can answer for our age and the architectural appearance of Moscow.

"Perhaps he doesn't know Moscow very well, like me with St. Petersburg, so he won't notice," I tell myself, soothingly.

"Where is my wife-to-be?" he demands and suddenly flies into a rage. "What a show they've put on, those bastards! Leaky great saucepans on wheels, boxes as high as the sky, giant mummers running around without stilts! It's not carnival week, damn it all!"

We're nearly at my block. I just need to get him across the street. I take our great author forcefully by the arm and drag him across the road where the traffic jam has still to build up so that the cars aren't slowing down and we have to make a dash for it. With trembling hand, I take my key ring from my bag and use the swipe key for the door to the entrance hall. It beeps and I go in, hauling Pushkin after me. He doesn't resist as though he's in a state of prostration.

"Goodness me, what have you got there?" asks the concierge as I wait for the lift. I give her an angry glare.

As the lift doors part, Pushkin muses quietly, "I'm in Hell. I was to be expected."

Once in the lift, to bolster his courage, I recite: "And to the people long shall I be dear… a Kalmyk, friend of the steppes." The lack of reaction suggests he has still to write these particular lines.

"We were led to believe that one plummets into Hell but Hell turns out to be on high as well and I had the temerity not to believe in it," Alexander Sergeyevich pronounces ruefully as we ascend.

"This isn't Hell, it's life," I say, aiming for a cheery tone. If I can just get into the flat, sit on the sofa, ply him with tea or wine, I'll be able to take my time to explain it all in detail.

"The Ancient Greek pagans had Charon, who was a man. Orthodox Christians have angels to conduct them to Paradise, which means this has to be a devil even if it doesn't have horns or a tail," Pushkin mutters, giving me a wary, sidelong look. He has evidently stopped seeing me as a person. I insert the key into the lock and usher my guest in first.

"No fires, just a confined space. And a mirror so that escape into oblivion is impossible. Any minute now and they'll clap me in irons," says Alexander Sergeyevich, assessing his surroundings.

"Tea, coffee, wine, cognac?

He replies as though talking to himself. "Fancy that: these wretches serve cognac. I'm in a hell for aristocrats." He smiles. "And thank God for that. I wonder where they keep the furnace?"

"Alexander Sergeyevich, you are not in Hell. You're in the future."

"How many eyes does Satan have?" He counts the green and red lights on the TV, video, and the computer's surge protector. "Two red, two green. Two up, two down. That's devils for you!"

All of a sudden, he bursts into peals of laughter as he looks at the ceiling lamp, all made of crystal, its light bulbs shaped like candles. "The candles in the lamps are lit. The flames aren't real but they still cast light."

"You're in the future. It's 2006." I don't even know where to start to make him believe that what's happened is real. And he's laughing, desperate but defiant too, as if to say: "So what if I have? I still can't bring myself to converse with demons." I take the collected works of A.S. Pushkin from the book shelf. This must interest him surely? It's got the publication date too. That should convince him.

"So Hell is the future? I understand, finally, I do. The future is Hell. Hell is the future. The Book of Revelations. The Whore of Babylon – is that you?" He addresses me at last.

I show him *The Tale of the Priest and his Servant Balda* but it makes no impression whatsoever. "Or are you a demon who has dragged my works away to your hall? The priest did warn me, blockhead that I am. He said, 'Alexander, Servant of God, you are doing the devil's work.'"

I take my own book from the shelf and point to a photograph.

"That's me. I wrote this."

"A portrait-miniature, on card, brush strokes effaced, the whole varnished. You even have artists working in your halls of Hell."

I am unable to explain what a photo actually is. I can see, however, that nothing surprises Pushkin any more. He's developed a theory. Even when I switch the TV on, he doesn't bat an eyelid.

"Ah, ha! Everything's been chopped into pieces and now they're burning in the fiery pit... Even Vasiliy Andreyevich Zhukovskiy used to tell me that hellfire is like the burning bush: nothing in it is consumed by fire and yet it is eternally aflame. Souls are hacked to pieces and stirred together like fruit in punch then tossed into the everlasting fire. Together with poems and pictures, with everything we've created. Was I shot? Was there a duel instead of the wedding?"

"No. You'll be shot later. You're still alive, you just happen to have come to the 21st century."

The phone rang.

"A bell. The summons to receive a fresh victim. So be it. The more the merrier. As long as it's not that Thaddeus Bulgarin.

I lift the receiver. It's Rosa. I say, "Please don't pass out but I've got Alexander Sergeyevich Pushkin sitting on my sofa. Can you get over here right away?"

Until now, Rosa has believed what I've said but now she decides I'm having her on. "You're not having me on? Are you seeing things?"

After that conversation, I think, 'No-one'll believe me. I'll say it's a hallucination. No, better still, a fantasy.'

Pushkin meanwhile is looking at me challengingly, rubbing his hands in obvious glee.

"I see it now: I've been taken to the lunatic asylum. You talk to yourself as if you're having a conversation! I do the exactly the same only I do it on paper. That's why Natalya Nikolayevna's parents have brought me here. That's why they've prevented our wedding. They think I'm crazy. I talk to myself in writing. I'm not in Hell and you're not a devil – you're Mad Meg."

I point to the television and turn on the sound.

"So what's that then, Mr. Pushkin?"

"They must be other people who are mentally disturbed, who have lost their reason and their minds, but since I myself am now an idiot, I see them as if they were hidden in a little box. It's just as well they did call off the wedding.

'To lose my mind I dread; 'tis worse

Than, facing beggary and dearth.'

The thing I feared the most has come to pass."

I had one argument in reserve, the most persuasive one. I switched on my laptop, drew up another chair and invited Pushkin to sit next to me at the desk.

"The desk is like mine and so is the mess," he observed, ignoring the computer booting up. In theory, I would have thought that an inhabitant of the century before last would have swooned in fright, amazement, or delight when confronted with unfamiliar objects then start to ask questions about electricity and the world-wide web but what Pushkin didn't know, he simply couldn't see.

"Perhaps it's a dream," he exclaimed, brightening when I opened an empty word document. "I'm dreaming about a luminous board — a tablet — on which letters will begin to appear. Will it be a divine message for me?"

I typed: "To Pushkin". He read out: "To Pushkin." I typed: "My dear Alexander Sergeyevich! The programme has crashed," I wrote. Then I deleted it. "An unspecified error has resulted in your being transported into the future to 2006 A.D. You are not in the underworld. You have not gone mad. You got married without a hitch and you will go on to have four offspring. With apologies for the inconvenience caused. You are my guest. This is not a dream. Our spelling's changed."

"Is this the word of God?" asked Pushkin.

"In a sense." I was already contemplating how to return the errant poet to his own time. Pushkin, however, did not vanish the next day nor indeed did he vanish at all. I raced off to the Pushkin Museum but no, nothing there had changed. That Pushkin lived out the life we all know, ended by a shot from D'Anthes, but now something had to be done about the other one.

Gradually, he stopped standing out. We bought him jeans, tee-shirts, and a jacket. No-one believed he was Pushkin. At a poetry evening I organized for him, he was heckled and booed and told it would never work and I was a dreadful manager. Gradually, Pushkin lost faith in himself and began to just loaf around because he was no longer fit for anything else. He didn't learn to use a computer. The slow drawl of his accented Russian was an irritant. He didn't understand was a telephone was. Everybody took him for some crazy *Gastarbeiter*. He couldn't obtain any papers or register in Moscow and it wasn't long before he was murdered. Not in a duel but by a gang of skinheads who shot him down in the street like a dog.

It proved no easy task to bury an illegal immigrant.

"He can be buried where he came from," I was told.

A bribe smoothed the way but no one I knew ever realized why on earth I was bothered about the little man who thought he was Pushkin. And they've regarded me with suspicion ever since.

Rosa was the only one who would go to the funeral with me. I had told them both — Rosa and the short-lived derivative of Pushkin — about something that happened in 2005. An American made unimaginable amounts of money on the stock exchange in just a single day by guessing all the share prices. He was arrested. He told the police he'd come to New York from the future where he'd got hold of a financial newspaper for 2005, which was how he knew it all. Of course, they didn't believe him but nor did they come up with any alternative. They promised to publish their findings after a thorough inquiry but they never did.

"We know everything that was in the past and nothing about the future," I said. "It's as if we're fixed to our own time with superglue and only making our way into the future with baby steps, on all fours, one day at a time, with all of eight hours of rest a day from the travails of the journey. Rosa, you've spent more than 30 years in a lethargic sleep. You sprang right into the future after that record leap through time, so why don't you believe that Alexander Sergeyevich Pushkin made an even bigger one?"

Rosa replied phlegmatically, "Because I'm the real me and the real Pushkin lived from 1779-1837. The personality doesn't turn out multiple copies like a printer."

"I once took my Pushkin for coffee at Café Pushkin on Tverskoy. It was right at the start," I reminisced. "And he yelled at the waiter, 'Waiter, do you recognize me?' It was really awkward and we had to beat a hasty retreat." I also remember how hard he found it to breathe. He said Moscow's air was toxic smoke and he was always coughing.

CHAPTER 2:
TIME RUNS AMOK

Isaac Newton filled 4,500 pages and spent 50 years calculating the date of the end of world – the result was the year 2060. In the Mayan calendar, the "end of the sun" falls in 2012 (on either 21 or 23 December). Someone with a love of symmetry amended it to 20.12.2012.

A lot of people think about dates in general because there is a significant but inexplicable link between numbers and life, between numbers and history. In the past, numbers were used only for sequencing. When there are only a few houses, they are given names, like the house of a friend of mine in Malta – the Villa Mozart – or the one behind me (through the wall and over the stone ramparts of the German ambassador's) – that used to be called The Rostov House. People started being given numbers once the population topped six billion. They were given numbers because of money – a taxpayer reference number, bank account number, insurance policy number. Everyone became the bearer of a dozen number sequences. Then identity as a whole was given in digits. Names as such began to fall out of use only after 2010. True, there was an instance in 2005 when one loving mamma wanted to call her child a number, a five figure one I think, but she wasn't allowed. Her explanation of what she wanted was that lots of people had the same names and she wanted her child's to be unique. Because, if the first time someone is designated by numbers it is 12345, you can guarantee that all the other number-bearers will be 12346 or something but only that one person will be called 12345. Presidents would, of course, immediately come to blows in order to be numbers 1, 2, or 3, but when numbers triumph over words, sequencing itself disappears. As a result, it won't be possible to start a new calendar from 2013 even though it's what many people are counting on right now. It's nice to put verbs into the future tense: it means the future still exists and is waiting for us.

Numbers are regarded as sacrosanct. Any old person can be called Vanya or Masha but numbers must not be repeated. There is a mystical fear of numbers as when the number 666 crops up (something of the sort occurred in 1998 and again on 06.06.2006) or a millennium (the year 1,000 or 2000). The Russian for digit or number – *tsifra* – is an inoffensive word taken from the German *Ziffer*, while the French version — *chiffre* — means code in Russian. And they are all from the Italian, the Latin and, ultimately, the Arabic — *sifr*, zero, empty. I have found one period when numbers were used exclusively for counting. Gradually, they became the only thing of substance: everything unnumbered passes away, falls into disuse, is erased from memory, doesn't exist at all. Names are used for differentiation but only within the limits of the specific drama played out in each individual life. There's the curtain raiser (the baby said "Mama" for the first time today, noticed someone other than itself for the first time), suspense (the voyage between Scylla and Carybdis), the climax (the hero rewarded) and then — game over. There's a feeling it should be a circle (a spiral, really) but the circle has been broken. It's just an arc from birth to death and other arcs are like the dark side of the moon. That's what happens with names but not with numbers. Numbers are the code everything's written in. They're like a flight of steps, they lead somewhere: one step, five steps, or a hundred at a time.

There's something not quite right about reincarnation. It seems fine in essence but there's something amiss. The soul is incarnated then disincarnated. There's a new birth and, possibly, Nirvana. Peace. Emptiness. Nothingness. What sort of nothingness? Fools cannot understand nor those without belief in the Kingdom of Heaven comprehend but something isn't right. There is nothing hid that shall not be manifested. Let's wait for it to happen.

This parenthesis of thinking was induced when Pushkin, who left no number trail, consequently vanished without trace. The brackets squeezed my brain and little geysers of thought started gushing forth.

Rosa and I went to my place to hold the wake. She was still being spiteful about 'my Pushkin'. "Why not just admit you've taken a lover? So, he's a fugitive from the loony bin, a short-arse, a caveman – where's the shame in that? You fancy him, so fine. I would have sympathized, shed a tear but this… don't expect me just to repeat after you that he's Pushkin the poet!"

Rosa was getting on my nerves. She talks about reincarnation but, faced with the reality, she denied it.

"Reincarnations only occur after death. The soul can't enter the same body twice," Rosa snapped.

"Where d'you get that from?"

"Everyone knows that."

"The reality is right there in front of you. You just don't want to accept it."

Long before the calendar ended, whereupon it became impossible to say precisely how long before, Rosa and I went our separate ways because of Pushkin. It wasn't because he was so very precious to me but it bothered me that Rosa took herself as par for the course but not him.

Basically, it was chance that brought Rosa to my place. Her story appears to be as follows (after all, whose story can be taken on trust?). She was in hospital in a lethargic sleep; someone was paying for her to be there and she was being looked after but the guards were fed up, another incarnation of Russia had bitten the dust, and the hospital refused to keep hold of Rosa, who lay there, a motionless Soviet-era leftover. The old guard may have been paid to keep watch over Rosa but the new ones couldn't be bothered. But Rosa was lucky: she had a compassionate doctor. He didn't toss her out onto the rubbish heap. Rather, he handed her over for safekeeping to a scientist who was researching lethargy. In order to survive in the new circumstances, the scientist had resorted to private business. He began to exhibit Rosa for money, presenting her as a unique and mysterious object. In the end, one of the new Russians bought Rosa off him. It was the time when every member of the nouveau riche was endeavouring to stand out somehow, but he grew bored with his toy and sold her on to a gallery owner. The gallery owner used her in art installations and Rosa gained a degree of popularity. It's obvious why Rosa hisses when people touch her. During the period of her lethargy-induced wanderings, anyone might try to pinch her, maul her, prod her with a finger to make sure she wasn't just a doll. On one occasion Rosa got up and began to walk (it happened once in a while), right in the middle of a private viewing and the gallery owner took fright. He sold her to a psychic and then she ended up with some Very Good Friends of mine. I don't know why they took her. They're part of the in-crowd, well-off, with no children or pets. Perhaps Rosa was precisely the still and silent creature they'd been dreaming of: she was utterly low maintenance.

It was nearly New Year 2005. My Very Good Friends rang to ask a favour. They said they'd been invited to celebrate New Year in the highest circles. Their housekeeper would be away over the holidays and they were afraid to leave Rosa alone and unsupervised so could I have her at my place overnight? I was at bit uncomfortable at the prospect although I had seen Rosa a number of times. Okay, I thought, it would be scary if I were on my own but with the people I've got coming, it'll be fine. My Very Good Friends laid Rosa, decked out like a Christmas tree, on the mat in my bedroom, spread a thick sheet underneath her, put a pillow they had brought with them under her head, covered her in a blanket, and left. At around midnight, I hadn't even thought about the body in the bedroom. We were seeing out the old year with champagne. We were all agreed that the next year had to be a better one and were waiting for the midnight chimes. They rang out, we clinked glasses loudly, and turned down the TV. In the second's silence that ensued, there was a rustle and then Rosa appeared in the doorway. It was a shock to us all even me, although I knew that Rosa's body sometimes moved without her waking up. Now, though, her eyes were open. She was rubbing them and stretching herself awake. Then she came in and sat down. The life and soul of the party started telling me off for failing to introduce him to such a looker and immediately downed a glass in honour of the New Year that had got off to such a surprising start.

"This is Rosa," I said tensely. "Hello, Rosa."

"Hello," she echoed.

I introduced the guests. Rosa's black-eyed gaze circled them and she repeated:

"Kolya, Natasha…"

"I'm Tanya," I added.

"What? You don't know each other?" said the same life and soul of the party, gobsmacked.

"Don't know each other," Rosa repeated and I got the feeling she was savouring the words. I didn't know what to say next but Kolya took charge so that at no point during that New Year's night did anyone seem to notice that anything special had happened. Kolya joked that I was keeping a girl hidden away, which led him to certain conclusions. It was nearly six in the morning when everyone left and Rosa, of course, stayed behind. I asked her if she needed to sleep and immediately realized how tactless that was. However, in a perfectly ordinary tone of voice, she said she'd slept her fill. I'd got a bit used to her during the night. We began to chat. She spoke in an odd accent and made surprising errors in her speech. Her mind was confused. She kept talking about various people as if about herself. She talked nonstop but I couldn't understand a thing. I wanted to go to sleep. I suggested she watched TV but, myself, I switched off.

It was three in the afternoon when I woke up and Rosa was still sitting by the TV. We had breakfast. Her speech was slightly more coherent. Now, she was full of questions. I had one of my own.

"How old are you?"

"I don't know," Rosa said and thought about it. It was impossible to say how old she was from her looks.

My Very Good Friends had vanished into thin air and only rang in the evening to say that they weren't in Moscow and would be back the next day. They apologized. I told them Rosa had woken up.

"Don't worry," they yelled into the receiver. "She'll go back to sleep any minute."

Towards nightfall, Rosa really did start preparing for sleep. I offered her the sofa, not knowing whether she would go back to her state of lethargy. But she had begun leading a normal human life. When my Very Good Friends came to collect her, they were disappointed. To begin with, they took her back but before long they rented a flat for her, very close to mine. Rosa came to see me every day. She had imprinted on me the way a duckling assumes the first thing that moves is its mother. Rosa didn't assume I was her mother but I was her first connection to the wakeful life. Within a year she had fully assimilated and her accent had disappeared. But there was something I couldn't understand: Rosa never mixed with anyone but talked about herself as if she had lived many lives. Amid the deluge of stories, I gradually began to single out permanent characters. What's more, they included people I had met in real life: Iris, for example. I even wanted to get them together but Rosa refused. She wasn't interested in people at all. Having talked herself out in the course of a year, Rosa more and more frequently said nothing and seemed indifferent apart from the outburst over Pushkin, after which she disappeared — at the very moment that Pushkin shook up my understanding of time, the fundamental principles of existence crumbled away like plaster, and life was altered retroactively. Back then, I thought Rosa had disappeared and it was only as time went by that I realized I was seeing her every day. That said, time didn't simply go by: it wasn't just set in motion, it was allowed to run completely amok or else strained against its confines until it burst and positively bloomed, like a rose. Because all those people whose lives were woven into the pattern of my own in a way I couldn't fathom at the time were Rosa. At her last appearance, she went to the computer and showed me Iris's diary.

"Did you just hack into that?" I asked.

"It's easy," Rosa replied.

"Hacking into other people's computers is easy?"

"It's all just easy."

And that was that. Rosa left.

CHAPTER 3: LIGHT. IRIS.

"I could see in the dark. It left other people blind, feeling their way with the soles of their feet as though they 'd landed on the Moon, their arms stretched out before them as if in zero-gravity. In accordance with an ancient and now refuted theory, my eyes radiated light. Enough to be able to make out the black-grey-black cells in a tartan that appeared white, red, and yellow in the light. Probably, during the day, light accumulated in my head as if in a solar battery and was stored there all night. I could see because I wanted to make out the world into which I had sprung like a shoot from a seed, germinating in rich soil. But compared to a plant I was a bird and had torn myself away from my roots.

"The moment of birth might not have registered in my memory, which requires the ability to speak, but it wasn't severed from my essential self when the cord was cut. The moment itself was like an earthquake, a tsunami, like plummeting from the top of a waterfall. Somewhere there was a flicker of light, darkness yawned, a shock wave tossed me into air that prickled and abraded, my only safety line the umbilical cord – and it held. When the storm had abated, there I was utterly alone in the hoary desert. Perhaps I had travelled through space. Strange as it seems, the expanse I had entered was sealed. There was no way out as if it was all that existed. There was no point bawling but my mouth was stopped anyway as though I could have alerted someone and made my escape. All that remained was to take a good look, take an interest, take it on board.

"People circled around me in their own chaotic orbits. In their midst, I was no-one: all the knowledge that had filled me evaporated as rapidly as ether. It didn't apply in the present mode. "No-one" is a percipient entity that been promised that they will be given support and answers not in words but through some sort of intravenous injection. Just as long as that No-one keeps paying attention, even in the dark. The alternative is to yawn and sleep away a whole lifetime here (when "here" means in this building, in Moscow, on this Earth) and then there won't be any answers.

"I had been provided with a guide named Hormone. His task was to induct new recruits into the adventure of life using a formula tried and tested a billion times over. Hormone told stories, offering a selection like tourist trips, putting those who chose the same routes on the bus and sending them off to their destinations. He couldn't understand why not everyone was happy when they came back from these fabled lands. He was particularly surprised by the ones who stayed in their story and made it their permanent place of residence yet still cursed their fate and Hormone to the high heavens. That said, only humans think the world is worth so much.

"'Aliens aren't insectoid extraterrestrials. They are ordinary humans you haven't learnt to love,' was my guide's lesson.

"Now not even light helps to see. Without glasses, letters and numbers merge into grey streaks, trails left by tiny caterpillars crossing white paper highways. These appear to be the first things rejected once an alien word has been adopted, assimilated, appropriated (these are synonyms aren't they?) There's no longer any need for its cyphers, its constant notation and calculation. Codes are issued when there are secrets but now all that's left are riddles without answers. I stopped seeing in the dark after Hormone told his horror story. I began to avoid the dark, afraid even to stretch out my arms or feel my way with the soles of my feet like Picasso's Girl on a Ball."

Although Hormone wielded inexorable power over Iris, she did everything she could to reduce and diminish it, imagining Hormone as some swashbuckling southerner. It had taken some time but Iris had long since come to terms with the fact that various personalities lived inside her. On one occasion, she decided to give them names. The one Iris subjected to Hormone's tyranny was Lyudmila, the only incarnation to see the power of her hormones as her essential self. Iris assigned herself the role of secret agent, the detective whose duty was to expose the inexplicable multiplication of her personality or at least to discover its roots. It was why she went to study psychology and did her master's dissertation and PhD on the theory of incarnations although she then reached an impasse. It was what made her start a diary too, simply to keep notes on what was going round in her head – what if there was a sudden miracle, something clicked, and the doors opened? At the age of 30 or even 37, life had been eternal but now it was as if someone had whispered in her ear that there was a cut-off point. It was impossible to believe this was true but the law of biology is stronger than faith.

It was precisely when Iris was 37 that Hormone unexpectedly turned from an amenable, albeit turbulent, companion into a despot and tormented her initially with stupid questions and then with his horror story. Hormone asked Iris,

"Why do you have such a stupid name?"

"Do you really not know, Hormone? It's not my real name. I got it when I was seven. Iris means Not-Rosa.

That's why they called me that – in order to pull up Rosa's roots and plant Iris in her place. There were other options: Lily, Daisy."

"And there was I thinking that it was because Irina (Grk.) means peace, that it was to pacify you. Of course they forgot that Ira (Lat.) means anger. In the eye, the iris lets light into the pupil. It's what even the Earth looks like from Space. You're a regular Ira: you couldn't possibly just enjoy life with me out of simple human kindness. You can still see in the dark which means that you haven't seen your fill of this world, that you're afraid to tear your gaze away even at night in case you suddenly miss what's most important.

Hormone managed to persuade Iris that her unproductive search was the product of a methodological error. When analysis becomes bogged down, the arrow of love will hit the mark. And Hormone began his tale.

It was night time and they were sitting in the light of the table lamp and the blue glow of the moon, which always unsettled Iris.

"Draw the blind," Hormone instructed. Iris did as she was told. "Turn off the light." She pressed the button. "Tell me what you can see."

"An ashtray, a bottle of wine, a notebook, a pen."

"What else?"

"An empty chair."

"It's not empty. That's where I'm sitting."

"But you're not a person. You're Hormone. You can't sit."

"Fine, I'll get up and move away," said Hormone. "Now the chair really is empty. If you like, I'll ask the one man you can't say no to come and sit in it. Just once in your life you'd like not to be able to say no, wouldn't you?"

"I didn't say no to Bertrand."

"That wasn't you. It was Natasha. Natasha's a loving woman, devoted when it comes to men, even though she's completely independent."

"I didn't say no to the Magus."

"That was Lyudmila. You said no to Alyosha and you left Tolik and now, sitting here today in the grey of Paris, on 1 December, with everyone already making an early start on their Christmas preparations, you're going backwards and forwards over traces that lead nowhere stop. So, they lead nowhere so that's that. You have to change what you're looking for. Does it really matter who your parents were? Is it important where your father vanished to or who Rosa and Sylvaine or whoever are? Where's your life, Iris, since that's the name you've been given and what you answer to? Hey, Ira!

"What?"

"Good, you do answer. I was thinking you'd nodded off."

"Thanks to you, Hormone, I can't go to sleep, thanks to your chirruping. You'd be better off telling me a bed-time story since there aren't any books I haven't read. "

"Look at the chair."

"Why do you keep going on about the chair?"

"Any minute now a ray of light will appear on it. A ray of light in a realm of darkness."

The space above the chair really did begin to grow a little brighter, just a touch at first, but the light grew stronger as if someone was surreptitiously turning up a dimmer switch.

"Sit on the chair."

"There you go."

Hormone had never spoken to Iris in peremptory tones in the past. She wouldn't have listened if he had.

"So, now you're the one with the ray of light and what's more light with a capital L."

Iris was an owl [Sova. Russ.] She came alive at night and slept until midday unless the alarm clock managed to rouse her any earlier as sleepy, blind, and ruffled as an owl. All of a sudden, this aspect of her being acquired flesh in real life: Sovka stretched her neck, arms, and legs, her whole body stretched, gathering around a single point, the place that Hormone dwelt, and from which he had been speaking to her all this time. Although to Sovka Hormone seemed to have become so immense that he took up the whole of space.

"Once upon a time an Owl was sitting on a branch," said Hormone, beginning his story. "She had already counted all the stars in the sky, all the marks on the Moon, all the branches on the surrounding trees, and so she was seized with a sense of yearning and began to hoot at the sky: "Whoo-whoo-whoo," more and more full-throated, more and more heartrending. This was her song. Nature had granted her no lovelier harmony. The hooting sounds woke a buck hare in its nest, the doe and their young, a lark began its keening ahead of time, a pack of wolves howled, a wind rose. And then, a ray of light shone on the Owl and only on the Owl. 'It must be he who created everything on Earth. Since it isn't a sunbeam, who else could it be?' the Owl thought. And she wished he would take the shape of something familiar, something kindred – such as an Eagle Owl. And he did and he settled beside her on the spreading branch. His eyes were eyes of chrysolite, his tongue a gleaming ruby in a beak of pure gold. He was as priceless as gemstones from his head to his feet of jasper with talons of moonstone. And everything in him shone. The Owl didn't even pause to think. She opened her beak to meet his, driven by a quivering impulse that seemed about to burst into a brilliance of butterflies. It never entered her head to ask the name of the Eagle Owl, which had begun as a ray of light, because she believed she knew it. She sobbed in ecstasy. He said her song spoke louder than the nightingale's. That her neck, unlike the swan's, could conceal a kiss. That her feathers were nobler than the parrots' ersatz flamboyance. That the heron, no matter how long its straw-yellow legs, could not reach so high as the Owl. He was her Saviour. True, she hadn't needed saving before then, but now that the Eagle Owl had appeared, salvation was apparently essential – salvation from the multitude of stars, the marks on the Moon, and the branches of the surrounding trees.

Now she was delivered from the multitudes she had thought of as variety until she had counted them all, although the sole point of that counting had been a long journey towards knowledge that had been like scaling a rope ladder. But the vast number obtained had revealed no truth to the Owl. She had counted to a billion. Real billionaires could count higher. "It's not what you count that matters," they would say, "carrots, counting rods, stars or dollars. What matters is reaching the highest possible number." Despite her exceptional eyesight, the Owl could not reach that number nor make the stars, the marks, or the branches her own. But the Eagle Owl was hers and the Eagle Owl was the greatest treasure there was. He clasped her in his long toes, spread his great wings, and carried her off to the end of the Earth. She trembled like a tiny sparrow in his vast and shining wings. The end of the Earth, which the Owl had so longed to see, was a bare, black bluff, a bottomless black abyss below. While the Owl, for some reason, had imagined it as green and blooming, full of crunchy dragonflies and pink worms.

At the end of the Earth, the Eagle Owl began to pluck out the Owl's feathers and to watch as they flew, spinning, into the abyss, and disappeared from view.

"It hurts," she sobbed.

The Eagle Owl looked at her crossly and said she looked like a plucked chicken and he would immediately gobble her up. "Ha, ha!" he burst into demonic laughter.

"Who are you?" the Owl asked, noticing with horror that she was completely naked and the Eagle Owl now looked like a vulture.

"Who but Lucifer ever shone in the dark?" came the menacing reply. "Who but the Prince of Darkness can use light to seduce an Owl that sees better in the dark than in brilliant sunlight?"

For some reason the Owl asked him if he loved her. He told her that Space consisted of dark material and dark energy and that the light in it was vanishingly small. It was vanishing because he, the Prince of Darkness, sucked it up like a vacuum cleaner. He was a black hole with a rampant force of gravity and he had already sucked her in. She was already inside the darkness. Thereupon the Owl closed her eyes tight and flew off into the abyss even though she was very frightened. She flew along the Earth, which had its own gravitational pull, from its End to its Beginning, to the oak tree she called her own, and the years went by and her feathers regrew and she flew over seas and deserts and saw forests. There were fewer and fewer forests on Earth. They were being cut down to make paper to cover in writing but the Owl managed to see them in time."

Iris changed after that story. She even stopped talking to Hormone. She became rabidly opposed to him. The story had rubbed off on her. A new character separated itself off inside her – the Owl. It gazed with unblinking, yellow eyes straight into the soul of its companion, which was somewhere in the region of the solar plexus. Neither girl nor boy – Owl. Its beak was curved because it didn't gape automatically at the sight of bait the way a triangular beak did. It wasn't a long beak because it didn't scour the swamps for titbits, like a heron. A Wise Owl: that's what it looked like because it didn't chirp, it didn't warble, it didn't repeat what was said.

CHAPTER 4. A FIND. IRIS.

Sometimes, you just don't want to do anything. On one of those days when the grown-ups were out, Iris was mooching around the flat – she'd made tea twice – when she became ashamed of being bored and decided to do something useful. She would go through the storage space which her parents kept stuffed with all sorts of odds and ends. The vacuum cleaner and ironing board could only just be squeezed in. She took a huge enamel basin out of the bathroom to act as a rubbish bin and started piling in leftover bits and pieces: ribbons used to wrap presents, a broken plug, electric cables, a bent lampshade frame, a tin of long dried-up paint. She came across things that had been given up for lost altogether: a glass button, a spattering of beads, tiny items in sweet boxes and biscuit tins, badges, dice, an elaborate brooch without a fastener, a single cufflink. She spent ages burrowing among these illusory valuables. There was nothing you could actually wear even though taken all together it looked like a treasure trove. Iris carefully stacked the boxes up again: they weren't for throwing out.

A dust storm arose deep inside the storage space, making Iris sneeze when she had barely begun raking through the books and papers that lay there. Newspapers, her old school books, and once favourite books about how the mole got his trousers, a well-thumbed copy of

Pinocchio, theatre tickets from ten years ago (when, in 1966, she was five years old), a little book in French about *Pif le Chien* and next to it a small volume in a language she didn't know but immediately remembered. Everything in her froze at these last two finds. She began to shake the forgotten but oh-so-beloved volume, dusting it off. An ID card fell out:

Sylvaine Personne,
Date of Birth: 13 June 1961,
Place of Birth: Paris
Citizenship: République Française
Father: Louis Personne
Mother: Angela Personne

A photo of her as a little girl was attached to the box. Everything was written in French and, as if it were a dream, she began to remember her father, mother, a cosy flat, and her father's studio, laden with picture frames and canvases. He had taken her there once. They went past the Sorbonne. He waved to someone. They spoke French. They always spoke French although Mama had an awful accent that embarrassed her when her friends came round. Papa had an indistinct accent but it was there. She remembered taking a plane and reading Pif comics.

Just then, her parents turned up. They found her sitting on the floor in the hall surrounded by heaps of stuff, with the two books on her lap, and the identity card of some Sylvaine or other in her hand. She couldn't understand why her photo was on the card: "I've never been called Sylvaine but before the move to Moscow my name was Rose. Here I became Irina."

"What do you mean?" my mother asked sternly. "What kind of nonsense is this?"

My stepfather took off his shoes and shook the first snow off his coat. My stepmother and stepfather: my adoptive mother and her second husband.

"My father disappeared soon after our 'great journey', as he used to call it. I was always trying to get out of him when we'd be going home to Paris but he would say: 'Paris was just a journey, our great journey.' In Moscow, he started speaking Russian and I was taught the language for a long time until it became my own. I didn't even start school at the beginning but went straight into Year Two."

"What does this mean, I'd like to know?" thundered my stepmother Mum.

I hated her. I stood up and answered cheekily.

"That's what I want to ask you, my guardian. What's going on with this card and where's my real mother?"

"Right, that's it. Time to see a shrink," my stepmother muttered to my stepfather and led him off into the flat.

It wasn't the first time she'd tried to scare me by talking about a psychiatrist. Previously, the bogey-man had been a policeman. Sometimes, I forgot myself and treated my parents as if I were a respectful, even loving, daughter. In moments of truth, however, I couldn't agree to acknowledge them as my parents and called them my guardians, saying I wasn't living at home but in a children's home, I had such a sharp sense of unreality, of my origins having been fabricated.

"Put everything back and hoover up," yelled my guardian from her bedroom. I didn't even consider doing as I was told. My first task was to hide my precious finds. Otherwise, my stepmother Mum (that's what I most often called her to myself and when I was talking to my friend) would find them and throw them out. There was no point hiding them at home so I quickly pulled on my coat and tore out of the house. I had to go to my friend's, where else? But on the way, I began to be assailed by doubts. What if her mother found my mementoes and told mine – parents are all one tribe, all in cahoots – but there was no other option. On Sundays my friend might be out with a boy – she'd already started dating, whereas I just went to dances with my school-friends, or sometimes went skating with students I knew. Having a boyfriend would have meant forcing myself to make a choice. Even now I have problems making choices. I like it when I'm swept away on a wave, when an unseen force imparts acceleration. Relying on the will of the elements that slumber in the deep is also a choice and often not the best, but it's the only one I can acknowledge as my own.

My friend was home, alone, and feeling distracted so she was pleased to see me. Simply asking her to put the two little books somewhere safe didn't work. She couldn't wait to find out why I wanted to hide these completely "non-criminal" books, in other words not Solzhenitsyn or Maupassant (parents concealed him from their teenagers as wildly erotic). They weren't even in Russian. I told her they were my father's books and my mother and stepfather were bound to throw them out. Disappointed, she shrugged her shoulders: she had a bookcase full of her father's books and wouldn't have cared if the whole lot was thrown out. "That's good," I thought, "it means she won't let anything slip." And that evening I vowed to myself that as soon as I was grown up, I would find out what happened in my childhood. After all, nothing vanishes without trace. There are archives and people. They could be found although I couldn't imagine where I would look or what I might find. The leads went back to Paris. The only opportunity to get there, from a 1976 perspective, was by getting married. I decided I would definitely marry a Frenchman. And this was why my crushes were short-lived and never serious: I would only love a Frenchman. This thought calmed me so much that when they started "brain washing" me at home, I proudly went to my room, slowly slid the bolt home, and lay on my bed with Victor Hugo's "Les Misérables". In the lesson, I would have to retell a chapter of it in my own, French words. "How am I any different from Cosette?" I thought as I fell asleep.

CHAPTER 5: HYPNOSIS

My stepmother Mum persisted in trying to take me to see a psychiatrist but then decided to reverse tactics: she invited a freelance psychoanalyst and real psycho to come to us. This ungainly individual, whose small, black eyes bored into me seemingly out of shyness, would come round once a week. "I'm a doctor," he would say each time, his tone ingratiating, then await my confession. "I am entirely at your disposal. I'm here to help." Yeah, right! Could he really give me back what I was looking for? Gradually, I got used to him and stopped seeing him as an enemy. "I am going to hypnotize you and then you'll be able to remember," he offered once. Until then, I had just made fun of him and, when I went round to my friend's, I used to imitate his rasping voice and we would both fall about laughing. But I was inspired by this suggestion from Psycho. After all, it is interesting, wondering what's hidden in the depths of the subconscious! I tried with all my might to sink into a hypnotic trance but to no avail. "It will work if you trust me." And, then, one day it did. I was hypnotized and Psycho recorded it all faithfully on tape.

My voice sounded from the tape. "I'm Rosa. My Mama danced flamenco. She was from Seville. My father took me away all of a sudden. He said we would be taking a flight and it would be better than the funfair but I felt he was taking me away because everyone in Paris was living on the streets, it was the beginning of the revolution, and he was afraid for me. Papa was Portuguese. He idolized the poet, Fernando Pessoa. He himself was a painter – and a concierge. When we left the plane, Papa said we were in Moscow.

"'What's Moscow?' I asked.

"'The capital of Russia,' he replied.

"There were a lot of people at the airport who spoke a growly, sandpapery language I had never heard before. We got into a car and I saw the city, plunged into darkness. The city streets were as wide as boulevards. I could make out occasional cars that seemed to have been selected for their ugliness and houses lining the sides of the roads. In the morning, I saw that the houses were dilapidated and covered in century-old dust. Billboards and banners above the streets all carried the same advert – for the CPSU – and the fronts of the houses bore a cycle of outsized portraits. The residents of this seemingly over-inflated expanse should have been giants but the people walking along the pavements were quite normal, although they were shabbily dressed and didn't look straight ahead but down at their feet. It seemed as if I'd landed on another planet that went by the name of Moscow-Capital-of-Russia.

"We stopped outside a very tall building that looked like a cathedral with a spire. In the flat, Dad and I were greeted by a woman and suddenly they both started speaking that weird language. My father told me she was my mother. To begin with I thought it was a game, the funfair just carrying on, then I cried and asked to go home to Mama. The woman pretending to be my mother said I had to forget about Paris and never speak of it out loud because I had to go to school and not only would no-one there believe me they'd take me to the police as well.

"'Try to get used to being a Soviet child,' my father said too. He soon vanished.

"'It's because of your Dad's job,' explained my newly-minted mother. And then I fell asleep and I slept so long that they took me to hospital. Around me, everyone spoke the liquid language I had gradually learnt – it reminded me of soup now, with added noodles – but I couldn't say a thing. I couldn't even move a finger or announce my presence in any way. I could hear people repeatedly saying: 'lethargic sleep'. I heard my father's voice. He dropped by several times. He was called Sandro, although Mama called him Luis, and he sometimes corrected it to Lui-sh, the Portuguese way. His French friends called him Louis.

"I dreamed various dreams and my names changed too. Occasionally I woke up. People in white coats would race over, clapping their hands. They fed me a sweet, cloudy pink sauce they called *kisel* but there was nothing to keep me in that whitewashed space and I would return to my own world. I closed the curtain of my eyelids with their velvet lashes and there, in the wings, I lived my real life. Sometimes I was moved somewhere. I would take a step towards the fresh air and the fragrance of flowers but again see the tiled walls, the white coats, and my audience applauding. Then I would fly away from them in a plane of my own, better than the funfair. I just couldn't find my way home or find Mama although I travelled a great deal. Sometimes I heard the words: 'They're paying for her.' A cold object would be brought close to my mouth and they'd say, 'She's alive.' Not long ago, a woman's voice said, 'She's been in this state of lethargy for eight years now.'

"A man's voice replied, 'It can go on for longer. The record's 22 years.'

"'She's 16 now. She was born in 1961,' the woman responded. 'She's looks just like a child.'

"Remember she can hear us. Don't say too much,' the man cautioned.

"'Oh, get away with you.' The woman rustled her paperwork and left.

"I saw the cold object once. It was a tiny mirror. I glanced into it and got a real fright. My face was fuzzy and sleepy, like a blurred photo."

"That does explain things a little," said Psycho with a sigh. "Your mother told me you went to France with your father as a child. It was stressful and when you came back you were always asleep although it was only a short-lived episode. It does go to show, however, how vulnerable you are psychologically. What really upsets your mother is that you can sometimes be perfectly normal, cheerful and friendly towards her, calling her 'Mummy,' and then, all of a sudden, you withdraw, look daggers at her, and insult her by saying she's just your guardian and not your mother at all. What do you think about that? And, shall we drop the formalities?"

The analyst was fairly young, about 10 years older than me, and I had been flattered that he'd addressed me formally. Now here was this direct offer of friendship. I nodded.

"Everything you say will remain between the two of us. Your Mum needs a result. She's afraid for your future and wants to help you become more balanced."

"Sure, she does!" I said, pulling a face. "She's thinking about herself not me. There's no need to fear for 'my future'. We know that already: I'll either be a journalist or a historian. I really do have an inner traitor, though, a coward. I will never, not even at gunpoint, acknowledge my stepmother but that coward couldn't care less about the truth. He just wants things to be as cosy as possible. For everything to be nice, to be patted on the head and looked after. More than anything in the world, my inner coward is afraid of conflicts and arguments, of not being liked."

"So what, is this a male person then?" asked Psycho.

"No, it's not. We always talk about human characteristics as masculine, that's all - *she* wants to get all she can out of life, to live for today, she couldn't give a shit."

"Does she have a name?"

"Are you laughing at me, sir?"

"We've dropped the formalities."

"Yes, but I'm not used to it yet. So no more 'sir' then… It's no good, I can't do it. Is it okay if I still say it? (And I did, although the nickname Psycho stuck).

"It's your decision."

"In a nutshell, then sir, do you suspect I've got a split personality, schizophrenia?"

"I don't suspect you've got anything. I can even tell you about one illustrious person who had a great many different personalities."

When Psycho told me that person's name, I threw my arms round his neck and kissed his rosy cheek. He was talking about Pessoa, my father's favourite poet."

CHAPTER 6:
FERNANDO PESSOA

"I was studying Psychology at Leningrad State University," Psycho began. "I finished my post-graduate studies that year but I didn't submit a dissertation. And all because of a Portuguese psychologist who had written a thesis about different personalities co-existing in one person. He had come to the USSR in search of some the material he still needed. He believed all of us there suffered from split personalities."

"We've got three. We're split three-ways," I put in. "As the joke says: Soviet people think one thing, say another, and do something else again."

"Precisely. This Portuguese psychologist was writing a dissertation on the psychological state of people in totalitarian states, like Portugal in Pessoa's lifetime. He had learnt Russian specially and come up with a pretext to visit but when our department realized what the dissertation was about he was immediately expelled from the country. Our brief friendship meant I had to move to Moscow. There would be no more work for me in my specialist field in Leningrad."

I began to feel sorry for Psycho. He was almost like my own kin now. Like me, he knew Pessoa – no-one else did. That was the moment a plan occurred to me that I was quick to act on: I went to Leningrad, following in

Psycho's footsteps. I began a psychology degree. That's how entranced I was by the story of the Portuguese man. To Psycho, I said:

"Thank you, Pscyho. I have finally realized that I am a prisoner here or, alternatively, an exile, sent to the north from a sunlit valley with little white houses, carrot-red tiled roofs, and rows of vines disappearing over the horizon."

"How do you know?"

"I remember. I don't know where from."

"So, Fernando Pessoa was born in 1888 in Lisbon. His father died when he was very young, his mother married a consul, and they all three left for South Africa where his stepfather had been assigned. Fernando learnt English and even went on to write in English sometimes. At 17, he returned to Lisbon and never left the city again. His parents stayed in South Africa. Pessoa used a legacy from his grandmother to open a printing press but soon went bust. He managed to find work as a foreign correspondent for the *Commercio* business paper but he was still regarded as a foreigner in his own country. Over the course of his life, he earned a bit here and there from occasional translations. Pessoa wrote from a young age. He wrote a vast amount in different genres, storing it away in a great trunk that hasn't been thoroughly investigated even today. With the permission of Pessoa's sister, my Portuguese researcher rooted around in that trunk and discovered fabulous things. Only one small book of poems was published in Pessoa's lifetime, which is hardly surprising.

"The monarchy fell when he was 22 and the republic was headed by a general and then by Salazar, who introduced a one-party system and the rule of special forces and the military. He cultivated Portuguese nationalism and declared the Catholic Church the moral authority. When Fascism arrived in Europe, Portugal fell into line. Pessoa never accepted it so no-one wanted to publish him and gradually he was utterly forgotten. Not at all like the current situation here, with a whiff of scandal always hanging over banned artists and writers. Pessoa was simply no use to anyone. He was an introvert and a worrier so life cocooned with just his typewriter for company suited him. He had a girlfriend. They split up and he never married.

"Pessoa peopled his life in an unusual fashion. At 25, he discovered he had a second personality. He called it his teacher, Alberto Caeiro. Then Pessoa produced another character, Ricardo Reis, epicurean and stoic, as experienced by Pessoa, and then another – Alvaro de Campos, minstrel of sensuality. Pessoa wrote poetry under these three names, which he called heteronyms. Every educated person in Portugal today knows them all. Since the fall of the dictatorship, Pessoa's fame has grown by the day but the poet himself died in poverty and obscurity in 1935.

"My Portuguese colleague," Psycho continued, "learned from Pessoa's writings that he was inhabited not by three but by far more characters. Each had its own name and biography and different parents from the others. Some were well-known, others not. There was no consistency to their alternation. Any one of them might appear for a day or a week and then Pessoa would be filled with someone else who would remember only their own yesterday which might be a month or a year ago, but would know nothing about the real past. My colleague discovered at least 50 personalities that had inhabited Pessoa. The poet was like the Earth, inhabited by different peoples, some in contact with one other, others believing they were alone in the world. They were of different ages. Some were female even. Pessoa was properly aware of only three, the poets, because they were in touch with the same literary circle, in touch with the world, so to speak. Those around him regarded it as a literary game.

"Where's the real you?" they would ask. "You change all the time."

"I don't change. I travel," Pessoa wrote. His travels into his inner world were just as varied and instructive as if he'd travelled the entire planet. But he had no need to venture even outside central Lisbon.

"One of the native inhabitants of Pessoa's inner world was an astrologist. During the dictatorship, such occupations were banned and Pessoa didn't tell a living soul. The astrologist helped him write a history of Portugal. When my Portuguese friend came across these writings, he gasped – the date of the fall of the Salazar regime was given to the day and Pessoa had predicted the whole of Portugal's history until 2000 plus, which is pretty difficult to imagine but he did it all the same. My friend claimed that all the poet's predictions to date had come true. That is, not the poet's predictions but those of the person who made them."

"You know, Psycho (these days, I'd never be able to call someone something like that but you can do anything when you're young and the nickname didn't seem offensive), you've opened my eyes. How come I never imagined inner journeys even when I quoted whoever it was who said "man is a universe"? It's sorted: I'm going to study Psychology at LGU. Then I'm going to Portugal."

CHAPTER 7: ROSA

I have no-one to talk to, to tell how good my life is. That's the biggest drawback of my situation, having no-one to talk to. But there are benefits: I am not bound by my body, my age, my circumstances. I can travel freely and become whoever I like. Of course, it's easy to begin with. Then there are more and more sidelong glances and ulterior motives, aimed at me, the most beautiful of mortals, Elena, Helen, by name, which means "light" in Greek. I never have enough light, which is why I became Elena. I was not born a purpled infant but arose fully-formed before a mirror in a pretty dress.

Yesterday was my sixteenth birthday. I blew out sixteen candles on my cake and I was allowed a little wine. It was nothing special and it made my head spin. I was sitting with my parents and their friends at our dacha, which, after repairs and perestroika, was now a villa. It had always been luxurious but tasteless in the Soviet fashion, whereas now it was as tasteful as a French medieval castle. That's what Daddy's guests said. And his guests were always in power.

"Who are you?" I would ask my father.

He would answer, "A magus and a wizard," and go on to say, "In Russia everything happens in secret. Those who run the country are invisible and those who pack its streets, trolleybuses, and administration lead a secret life too. All that is manifest is false and organized so that no-one is able to see real life and thereby encroach upon it or disturb anything in it."

Since my father was a magus and a wizard, aides to the country's top people would come to see him, while those in the third and fourth ranks would come in person, asking what they needed to do next to ensure that no-one disturbed their secret lives. Here's what my father would said. "Die," he told Brezhnev. "Die," he told Andropov. "Die," he told Chernenko, and all because one secret had perished and another was on the way. For the secret that is gradually becoming known does die. The secret lion hunting has passed away as has the Mercedes collection in its secret garage. Wealth needs freedom if everyone is to come to the feast, the dacha to become a castle, and the whole of the city to shine because there is no more pleasure to be had from the exclusive consumption of black caviar. A new secret is hoving into view.

Everyone was afraid of taking the old secret apart and turning it inside out and at that point my father said to Gorbachev, "Stick two fingers down the country's throat and it will happily throw up and you'll be Time Magazine's Man of the Year, Man of the Decade even." And so it came to pass. But Gorbachev's delight was short-lived:

"What is to be done? Now the hungry are tearing me limb from limb and 250 million people bearing bludgeons, their secret lives also destroyed, are massing at the gates."

"Get out of here," my father said. "And do it as a hero."

And he came up with Foros and the State Committee on the State of Emergency so that Gorbachev could make a fine exit. That was when I had just turned sixteen and I became a beauty queen. Contests were being held all over the place. Without competition, the fields had become overgrown with moss and lichen, the houses covered with mould and people encrusted with scabies. The advent of the contests was like sunshine after rain. There was an injection of fresh blood so that I wasn't competing only against the daughters of those now known as VIPs but also against girls from humbler backgrounds. Everyone was as happy as children with the "wind of change" until it became a hurricane. Everyone hoped it would blow away the cobwebs from the place, and indeed from themselves. I began to blow my own cobwebs away, too. It was called a "world tour".

You wouldn't have known it was me. So much money and effort was invested in me – stylists, designers, fitness trainers, catwalk tutors, beauticians, dieticians, photographers, journalists, experts in biorhythms and the lucky days of the lunar calendar – that I became a work of art. During my first tour, I received air kisses, flowers, and heart-shaped balloons but, during my second eggs, tomatoes, mayonnaise, and custard pies were hurled at me and protestors unfurled banners declaring me the daughter of the grey cardinal who had driven dear old Gorby out of the Kremlin, saying that I was Russian Mafia and my beauty not Russian at all. So said Russia's new friends, while its old friends averted their gaze as though I was a traitor to Communism and the whole Arab world. And they swore vengeance to boot. "Look how he avenged his brother!" I thought, recalling the Georgian story about Lenin and my flesh crawled. At that point, my father said that all this was a price that had to be paid but the goal was for me to marry the US president and then our two countries would be related and together they would rule the world.

"You must do it," he told me, "for Russia. Especially since their president's a charming man."

"He's married," I protested but my father ignored my objections.

"I'll arrange things so that you can get to know him and he won't be able to resist your beauty," my father assured me. "The main thing is that it has to be a matter of public knowledge. There'll be a scandal. His wife will divorce him and the only thing left will be for him to marry you. Otherwise, he'll be impeached."

That's almost what happened. With just one difference: that the resounding and protracted scandal which almost led to both divorce and impeachment evaporated in the space of an hour and I was left feeling dishonoured in front of the whole world. After all, I wasn't an American who could make a million out of my shame then sit back and enjoy the high life. I couldn't go out. I hid my face, which was well-known even in the Australian outback. There was nowhere for me to go. In my despair that there was no longer a place for me even in space, I longed to sink through the floor and I did – I went back through so many centuries that America, Russia, and Europe had not even come into being.

Scattered between three seas, the Aegean, the Mediterranean, and the black Pontos, all the Greek city states, even as they lived their own lives and waged war on one another, knew that the universe had but a single centre – Mount Olympus. Granted, the *demos* had a rather clearer belief in their kings than in their gods but people said that things hadn't always been this way, that life had grown dull as it dimmed the light that shone on it and now it crept through the lowlands in search of a substitute for light that could be held in the hand – gold. I lived permanently divided, split between earth and sky, unlike my profoundly terrestrial sister, Clytemnestra. We were both daughters of Leda but my father was Zeus and hers Tyndareus, our mother's legitimate husband, King of Sparta. He was a good man. He gave us away in marriage to two orphaned brothers, Clytemnestra to Agamemnon and me to Menelaus. Everything went well while the brothers were orphans and refugees after Aegisthus killed their father, Atreus, and they fled Mycenae for Sparta. We were a family, a single unit, and we lived happily, telling one another what we knew of the lives of the gods and our ancestors. It wasn't as if Aegisthus just up and killed Atreus. Their line was long ago cursed by the gods in the days when people were still learning from the Olympians and had not yet defied them. Tantalus, however, decided that the gods were simply spinning him a yarn and decided to put their omniscience and omnipotence to the test. Since then, their line has been adrift in a relentless cycle of violence.

Eventually, we thought there was a lull in the fighting. Although Mycenae itself was in turmoil and our husbands were about to bring their homeland to its knees. But Tyndareus sorted even that out: he ensured that Agamemnon became the rightful King of Mycenae and Aegisthus was exiled from the city state. And so, my sister and I were separated – for the moment, by distance only. The ageing Tyndareus decided to hand power over to a new king and asked everyone to suggest the best candidate and Menelaus was chosen King of Sparta. That's when the trouble really started. Menelaus became a greater Spartan than if he'd been born to it and, as head of the city state, he engaged in furious activity. He trained the Spartans to be as strong, as brave, and as hardy as possible so that none of them would find themselves in his place – fleeing from tragedy in terror, in disgust at the rebel Aegisthus, his and Agamemnon's cousin. Menelaus created a great army and drilled it day and night. Meanwhile, I was dreaming more and more often of divine love. I knew what that was and what it should be like: when Zeus descended as a shower of gold and Danae shone with his golden light, when he took the form of a white swan and approached my mother Leda as she rested on the shore and her life became as light as his white feather down so that I have a swan-like neck and white skin despite the scorching sun and Clymtemnestra, by comparison, looks like a duck.

Once Clytemnestra had grown into her role as queen, she was beset by claustrophobia. She felt hemmed in by Mycenae, capital of Crete, by the whole of that vast island even, and she longed for power, for which read divine power, over the whole world. None of us imagined that there was another world in addition to Hellas and nature. Otherwise, it would have made itself known, called in on us in an alien ship. As it was, there were just rumours that someone, somewhere had seen little yellow people with round, flat faces and slits for eyes.

Clytemnestra became jealous of Menelaus and what's more it was because of me, because of my origins. She was consumed by the thought that Menelaus had more chance of becoming king of kings than Agamemnon: Zeus might offer protection to his kin even though I had never seen my father. Unperturbed, Menelaus put Sparta on a war footing, told its young men to sleep in sackcloth and hurl spears, and urged neighbours to pit their strength against one another and abandon feasting in favour of the tilting yard. As for me, I missed the sky and wings. The healthy mind in a healthy body imposed by Menelaus bored me rigid. The next thing I knew, Menelaus had made peace with Aegisthus and was saying let bygones be bygones. He liked the sound of Aegisthus's assurances that the family curse was an invention, that everything depended on individuals and nothing had been lost and the members of the family should therefore be reconciled and live in harmony. Aegisthus was an atheist. He didn't even believe in the battle between the gods and the giants when Zeus won people the right to be the most important, more important even than Gaia, the Earth.

Day after day, Aegisthus was doing the rounds, paying visits, holding conversations. There was nothing else he could do. Imperceptibly, he became the go-between between the city states and the islands, or so we thought. In actual fact, his sole aim was the throne of Mycenae. He was merely searching for a means to rid the world of Agamemnon. Murder was pointless since the way to Clytemnestra's heart was closed to him. He wasn't allowed even to step foot on Crete. Aegisthus lived at sea and slept on his ship. He crept towards the throne like a cat, claws sheathed, attempting to do anyone he could a favour.

Aegisthus became a frequent visitor to Sparta. He even went to Troy and advised Menelaus to issue an invitation to Paris, son of King Priam, in order to establish a rapport with that city out on a limb since Troy was rumoured to be fabulously wealthy, albeit old-fashioned too: the Trojans still honoured the gods and communicated with them on a daily basis. Menelaus liked the idea of inviting the Trojans over but it was Priam he wanted to see, not his younger son. Aegisthus exclaimed: "There is nothing Priam needs. Troy is a hundred times wealthier than Sparta. I barely managed to persuade him to send his son to Sparta, the younger one because the god Ares has acknowledged the eldest, Hector, as the greatest warrior in the universe and Priam won't let him make the dangerous crossing. And he got married recently too whereas it's just the right time for Paris to see a bit of life." Who could have known at the time that, during his visit to Troy, Aegisthus would use me to lure Paris, me and, as he stressed in particular, my heavenly beauty? Paris even secured Aphrodite's blessing for his journey to Sparta although the other goddesses vied with one another to dissuade him. "It's not surprising," Paris thought at the time, "after all I did award the apple to Aphrodite. The others were probably upset."

Paris left for Sparta. Menelaus prepared for his arrival with singular pomp and circumstance. He ordered enough goose liver paté to be made as would fill a cup for ritual ablutions. He ordered plaice to be caught, each the size of a plate. This guest wasn't about to marvel at feta and aubergines. Menelaus, however, hung back in Mycenae for some reason. He had sailed to see Agamemnon so that he could bring the whole family to feast with the Trojans. Later it turned out that he had taken Aegisthus to make his peace but the mission failed, everyone squabbled, and time stood still as far as reconciliation went. Perhaps that was also part of Aegisthus's plan. Paris arrived while Menelaus was away. Would that I had never set eyes on that foreigner! The most handsome of mortal men brought with him Eros and his quiver of arrows. I was fated not to dodge a single one of them. I eloped with Paris on his ship, in secret, at night, during a storm.

Aegisthus took Menelaus who was inconsolable under his wing. He advised him to unite the Achaean armies so as to take Troy the Unassailable by storm. Agamemnon set a condition, which Clytemnestra had whispered to him: he was to be commander of the Archaean armies. Aegisthus had been expecting this: the commander of the troops was the one who would ride out ahead of them all, which meant Agamemnon was almost certain to perish. What could he do against Hector, after all?! This crafty cousin also sent an oracle to Agamemnon. The oracle ordered Agamemnon to sacrifice his most precious possession, a down payment to the gods for victory. His most precious possession was Iphigenia, his and Clytemnestra's youngest daughter. Agamemnon needed victory at any price and the fewer the chances of getting what you want, the greater the readiness to make sacrifices. The oracle was consulted about causes that were already lost. The oracle had also been sent with Clytemnestra in mind. In the twinkling of an eye, she came to hate her husband, when she saw him holding a bloodstained knife used to slaughter sheep. The blood it dripped with was Iphigenia's. No matter how

Agamemnon assured her that Zeus had taken Iphigenia to heaven and a lamb had been slaughtered in her stead, Clytemnestra shrieked that she didn't believe in stories, not even the one she had known since childhood that claimed I was born from an egg, and that it was ridiculous to think our mother could have been seduced by a swan, even if it had been as beautiful as Apollo.

In this way, Aegisthus reconfigured space to his own advantage.

From Sparta, where ascetism and barrack-room culture prevailed, I came to the magnificence that was Troy, with its marble floors, inlaid, fine wood ceilings, statues of all the gods and goddesses, columns with pure gold capitals. The Trojans themselves struck me too – they smiled when they met you and seemed to be happy. All bar Cassandra, Paris's sister. "What sadness is eating her?" I asked but Paris said it wasn't sadness but a clouding of the mind. "She thinks she's clairvoyante and prophesies all manner of woe for Troy. When I went to Sparta, she said it would mean the death of Troy and that Hector, father and I and nearly all the Trojans would perish.

"'Are you going to die too then?' I asked her.

"In the same minor key she replied, 'No, I'll live.'

"Prophets are prepared to dispatch the whole world to the underworld except themselves. The only thing Cassandra got right is that I would bring you back from Sparta. That's no surprise. The rumour of your beauty had reached even our walls."

Paris and I were married. At the wedding, Cassandra was as morose as she was every other day and, instead of congratulations, declaimed: "The war has started. The army is on the move." She spoke so bluntly that I felt uncomfortable but King Priam stroked her head and soothed her like a small child, saying, "Troy is surrounded by such a high wall that no horse can leap it."

"A horse will," Cassandra retorted despite all the evidence.

"Even if someone does wage war on us, Hector is the best warrior in the world," Priam continued to remonstrate.

"That's why he's the best, so that he can fight," the girl persisted, by no means calmer. "And if someone is the best, his equal will be found."

She was led away from the wedding with difficulty and as she went she cried out in a terrible voice: "Troy will perish because of her, because of Helen." All the many members of Priam's family beseeched me to forgive the hapless girl and the wedding banquets lasted a whole week. Everyone, apart from Cassandra, treated me with love and respect because I was also the daughter of Zeus and the Trojans worshipped the Olympians.

A month went by in languor and oblivion. Not once did I think of Menelaus, or my sister Clytemnestra, or even of Aegisthus by whose good graces I had come to Troy. And then the sentries on the tower were hit by arrows and, through a peephole, I saw thousands of spear-bearing riders who turned out to be the combined Achaean army. Menelaus was there and Agamemnon. The siege of Troy continued for ten years. Achilles slew the world's best warrior in battle and a wooden horse was brought into Troy as a gift. Out of it leapt a multitude of Achaeans who killed both Paris and the king. Of the whole family, only Cassandra and I were left. Agamemnon took Cassandra prisoner and Menelaus took me. For seven whole years when the war was raging, Aegisthus ruled Mycenae, having married my sister. They murdered Agamemnon, the unexpected victor, but did not survive him by much. The revenge of Agamemnon's son, Orestes, was swift. The curse of the gods remained effective to the end of Tantalus's line. Zeus protected his daughter. I lived and Menelaus forgave me. He even came to believe that I had never left Sparta, that it was my spectre, my double, my heteronym that had appeared in Troy. After the war, the world was changed. All lands united in the single state of Hellas and only then was it discovered that beyond its borders lay Persia, India, and the little, yellow-skinned Chinese and this is all that consoles me, that I changed history for the better, without even trying.

When I came round and was back in our own time and our own country, I told my father,

"History these days can only be changed for the worse."

"So I have a Cassandra of my own," my father replied and I remembered just what an insufferable person she'd been.

CHAPTER 8:
THE PSYCHOLOGY DEPARTMENT

"What a relief to start life over again from scratch! Nobody in Leningrad knew me and I knew nobody there. The little I took with me included, of course, my precious books, Pif and the little book of Pessoa poems in Portuguese – the material evidence of my identity. Thanks to Psycho, I was already familiar with that kind of vocabulary and I easily got a place to study psychology.

It was only the students in our department, from the third year onwards, who could read Freud and then only in the library. Everyone had heard of him but nothing could be found out about him apart from vague mentions in Yaroshevskiy's "A History of Psychology". Nobody at all was allowed to borrow Jung but I even managed to do that too. Actually, I was able to do an awful lot thanks to Alyosha. He was a history student three years ahead of me and a wunderkind – the star of the university. He knew several languages. He had an amazing collection of books and he knew everything. At least, everything I might ask: Freud, Jung, Shibutani, Gurdjieff.

I devoured Shibutani's social psychology like a detective story. We are mirrors of one another. We're not selves, we're reflections in the eyes of others. My parents told me I was a well-behaved, obedient child and a loving daughter known as Sovka, and so I was. Or else I was anti-Sovka, rude, disrespectful, a regular tearaway. Only those two versions were ever used on my parents. Here in Leningrad, though, everything changed. I was called Ira. People saw a brunette femme fatale, half-gypsy (at a stretch, my external appearance could be explained by having a Georgian father), proud and mysterious. That's how Alyosha saw me. The others followed suit. I rapidly began to approximate to that image. My spine straightened out of its own accord. My shoulders went back in pride. My gaze became vampish – in other words seductive but cold. Out of all the female students – and they were all in love with him – Alyosha chose me.

He was predicted to have a future as a great historian. In addition to his exceptional learning, he had beauty, eloquence, refined manners, and impeccable taste. He was the epitome of the Silver Age, a veritable Alexander Blok. We were inseparable and parted only after midnight as the bridges began to open. Only the rising halves of the bridges could tear us away from one another. After university, Alyosha was sent to Moscow for post-graduate study. He left for the capital before we had time to get married although we had applied to ZAGS, the civil registry office. Registered as a resident in Leningrad, I had no right to live in Moscow whereas Alyosha had a temporary permit for the duration of his studies and a place in a hostel. It was too prestigious an offer to turn down. I supported him in that but we didn't see much of one another anymore. Alyosha would visit Leninburg as he called it and I went to Moscow for the holidays, but it was impossible to get any privacy in the hostel and we both suffered from the enforced separation. I attempted to transfer my course to Moscow but in vain. Alyosha found a way to get me there, though. He had made friends with a Muscovite, a young scientist, who agreed on a fictitious marriage with me so that I would have a legitimate reason for moving to the capital. I didn't want to abandon my studies so we had to wait another two years. That time passed differently for each of us. He found my not being there difficult. His dissertation wasn't going well. He couldn't focus and preferred just killing time with friends since he always played first fiddle in any group and he liked that. Alyosha lost his place in the hostel when, after three years as a post-graduate, he'd made no progress on his dissertation. He moved into the studio of an artist, one of his new friends. It was always swarming with people. Studios were impromptu clubs in those days. People would just drop by. They told me there were two things about Alyosha that cast a spell: his erudition and his tales of the Beautiful Lady, i.e. me, depicting me as the very best of all the women who had ever lived on this earth so that when they met me these people were ever so slightly disappointed. For my part, I meekly carried on studying and when I got my degree I was obliged to work in my specialist field for another three years. My move to Moscow was being endlessly deferred.

Alyosha's friend, Tolya, who had agreed to the fictitious wedding, was finally introduced to me. He was Alyosha's polar opposite. Not only had he submitted his thesis and was working at a scientific research institute, he was also earning good money – he wrote research papers for slacker students, all originally from the southern Soviet republics (although these days nearly all students are like that). In the USSR, people's proper, what you might call their legitimate, work, earned them a pittance. And not much has changed now either. Tolya had a flat of his own. He was passionate about his subject – genetics – and we were attracted to one another at first sight. Alyosha was living with other people at their expense. He was too old to be a wunderkind but people still had high hopes of him and, aware of his situation, expected my move to

Moscow to restore his ability to work. Alyosha, however, had become accustomed to his role as a master of rhetoric and fine judge of the arts, for whom everyone was full of admiration and had the sympathy reserved for any Romeo: poor boy, he simply couldn't wait for his Juliet to arrive but had nowhere for her to live and nothing to give her to eat. Alyosha hoped everything would sort itself out but Tolya came to Petersburg and bought me a document, excusing me from having to work, on the grounds that he was taking me away to Moscow to be married. So our marriage wasn't fictitious at all. Alyosha realized this the moment the marriage was solemnized and it came as a terrible shock. He and I carried on meeting up, however. When I went to see him in the studio in which he had taken shelter, I sincerely believed I was going back to him for good. As I went home, I knew I would carry on living with Tolya. My relationship with Alyosha was now a secret from Tolya. It used to be the other way around.

Time passed and Tolya found out everything. He didn't throw me out, though. Now they both waited, like rivals, to see who would win. No-one did. Alyosha was so very much the artist and I'd got to know the most interesting people in the Moscow art world because he was friends with them all. Tolya was an introvert. All that kept us together was our home while the big wild world sailed past somewhere far away. But being with Tolya was like being behind a stone wall and losing that fortress was terrifying. The situation was coming to a head and on one occasion Tolya and Alyosha met and agreed to give me an ultimatum: I had to pick one of them. It was torture! My whole life I've never been any good at making choices. I go into a complete stupor when I have to make one. It made no difference that I'd exchanged my nice St Petersburg apartment (in those days flats weren't bought and sold, they were exchanged) for a one-room flat in a Moscow commuter town. I decided I needed to be alone.

It was just at that time that political changes began. Foreign journalists flooded into Moscow and St Petersburg. Embassies opened for a new generation. I was caught up in that wave. I made the acquaintance of a French journalist. We embarked on an affair. I became pregnant. I still don't know whose baby it was. Because when the ultimatum expired and before I'd made my decision, both Tolya and Alyosha started asking me to come back. Everything had gone full circle except that there was now a third man involved. Once again, I couldn't make up my mind. Alyosha and Tolya were torturing me to find out who got me pregnant. I told them both I didn't know but they were both convinced I was saying it deliberately, plotting something. They didn't know there was a third man. He was married at the time but suddenly offered me his hand and heart. He decided to divorce and that I should do the same. So I did. Tolya decided this meant I'd chosen Alyosha and was expecting his baby. It's what Alyosha thought too. He was in seventh heaven and didn't listen when I told him he was wrong. My new love interest, Bertrand, divorced fairly quickly. Marrying Russian women was fashionable and prestigious back then. We married and I left the country with him. Of course, it was a purely Soviet story: a residence permit, love affairs out of sheer boredom, marriage to a foreigner... I lied to Bertrand that it was his baby although I knew for certain that it wasn't. It was either Tolya's or Alyosha's. Then a terrible thing happened and I began to be afraid of lies."

CHAPTER 9: NATASHA

Back in Moscow from Paris in the summer of 1992, Iris rang Psycho. She couldn't bring herself to talk to anyone else. He, at least, would listen to what she had to say.

"So, how's it going in France? I'm pleased everything's worked out for you," said Psycho, welcoming his friend. "How many years is it since we last met? Three? Four? Are you back in the land of your ancestors for long?"

Psycho didn't believe Iris when she said she was back in Moscow for good.

"Don't even think about it," Psycho said, waving his arms. "There's nothing but blood and filth here. I'm thrilled to bits that the evil empire has come crashing down but life for the garbage in the dustbin of history doesn't hold out much hope for the garbage."

"I'm garbage," Iris replied, almost shouting "I don't even know who I am. I'm no-one. I don't exist! Something terrible's happened."

"Some drink their cup of horror when they're young. It's served up to others at the end of the day. Yours is the kind that's never empty."

"You're not joking. My personality keeps on multiplying. When Bertrand and I moved to Paris, I acquired yet another name. The fact that I was Russian attracted attention. People didn't know much about contemporary Russians and when the people Bertrand knew were trying to establish my identity they remembered the Gilbert Becaud song 'Nathalie'. 'You're Russian? Nathalie. Red Square.' Even Bertrand called me Natasha despite the fact that it was the name used by the prostitutes pouring out of the former Soviet republics. For various reasons and in various contexts, it came to mean any 'good-looking Russian woman'. I quite liked my change of name. I wanted with all my heart to have done with my old life and to embark on a new one."

"Just be aware," Psycho put in, "that that's always been what you've wanted. You're Russian to the core despite these allegedly Latin parents of yours. I'm getting the feeling you've found out a lot of interesting stuff about them."

"I haven't. I stopped thinking about the past altogether. I became a model Nathalie: an attentive wife, a real mother hen, founder of an association of Russian Parisians from all the waves of emigration. We began to publish a newspaper. It had a small print-run but it was in French so that the French could get to know our culture better or rather could get to know us, real live Russians, better. We were the ideal couple. Russian-French marriages sprang up like mushrooms in the soil of Gorbymania but all the ones I knew either fell apart or didn't work. Expectations were too high on both sides: the Russian woman was an ethereal, romantic Natasha Rostova, the French man represented prosperous good living. Consequently, Natasha Rostova insisted on luxury, accusing her husband of being like Balzac's Gobseck or Pushkin's miserly knight, while he tried to be shot of her as soon as possible so that she didn't get even a centime when they divorced. We were nothing like that. I wanted a real family, without any disturbances or multiple personalities. I wanted to live a long and happy life with Bertrand and then die on the very same day. That's almost what happened.

"I was wracked with remorse over our son's paternity. I would behave with exaggerated virtue to try and put it right, to cancel out the lie that was living with us. Our son was getting bigger and my feeling of dread increased. He was the spitting image of Tolya. People around us threw oil on the flames, saying he didn't look like either his father or his mother. Every one of these comments would make me blush and I would start rabbiting on about children who don't look like anyone turning out to be geniuses. Meanwhile, my head thumped with the question: what if Bertrand suddenly sees a photograph of Tolya or even sees Tolya himself? At some point, rather than just being nicknamed Natasha, I became the real Natasha. Without a past. Forgive me, Natasha, you're not me. You really were a model of integrity."

Psycho looked quizzical.

"Who are you talking about?"

"Listen to what happened next. Bertrand, the child, and I were going on holiday on the Cote d'Azur. Bertrand had decided to go by car. It was a thousand kilometres but he reckoned it would work out cheaper than going by plane or train and then getting a taxi. And if we had the car we could do some travelling. Bertrand did the driving and during the final third of the journey, near Marseilles, he said he was tired. We went to a motorway café, had some coffee, and our little boy, who was usually so well-behaved but must have been bored with the long journey, started playing up and complaining that he wasn't going any further and when his father shouted at him and clipped him round the ear, he hit him back, and called him something really obscene in French. And that's when it started. Betrand hit the roof. 'Just who are you like?' he yelled.

"'Not you. I don't want anything to do with you,' the furious child retorted. We dragged him towards the car, both of us really wound up, especially Bertrand, and

I suggested that I drove. I'd passed my test by then. They kept on arguing in the car. I wanted to get there as quickly as possible so I put my foot down, overtaking everyone. There weren't all that many cars really... Natasha died instantly. The boy a week later in hospital. Bertrand received a blow to the head. His mind never recovered."

Tears streamed down Iris's face.

"I'm sorry but I just can't handle this. Do you understand what happened, Psycho?"

"I understand what happened but who are you talking about? Which Natasha died?"

"I did."

"But –"

"Yes, me. Me. Natasha is me. Only I'm sitting here with you and she's dead and buried."

Psycho didn't immediately know what to say but he did understand that Iris's defences had gone for good.

"Go on."

"I came round in the hospital. They told me I had concussion, that there'd been an accident, what we call an RTA. They asked for my papers. I didn't have any. I gave them my name and address and asked what had happened to Bertrand and the boy. The doctor promised to find out. A little later he came and told me that the woman whose name I had given was dead and her husband and son were in hospital in Toulon."

"'But you are in hospital in Paris,' he added meaningfully. 'You were knocked down by a car as you ran across Avenue Mac Mahon. You didn't use the crossing. You've got off lightly. You'll have a bad headache for two or three weeks. I need your insurance policy. Then I'll tell you how many days we can keep you free of charge'"

"There was a re-run of the previous dialogue about my son, Bertrand, my address, the two separate accidents in Toulon and Paris."

"'I'm bringing a psychiatrist in,' the doctor said.

"There was a second re-run, then a third – with a police officer and an investigator. Each one of them went on to say, 'Besides, you say you're Irina Portier. The dead woman was Nathalie Portier.'

"There was a Soviet international passport in my jacket, three hundred francs, and a packet of tissues. My handbag was probably lost in the accident.

"'Where were you going in such a hurry?' the police officer asked.

"'The seaside,' I replied."

"What did the psychiatrist say?" Psycho asked cautiously.

"The psychiatrist concluded that I'd suffered partial memory loss in the crash. That Nathalie must have been my friend and I was experiencing her death as if it had happened to me."

"It's feasible," Psycho said, with a sigh. "So where did you go when you left hospital?"

"The police took me to the Russian Embassy where the dialogue had a fourth re-run. I rang my friends from there. They all knew about the accident already. I would start talking and they'd be overcome with horror and throw down the receiver. The embassy explained that Bertrand had now been moved to a Paris hospital and kindly agreed to take me there. The ward sister warned me he'd had a complete breakdown. I went to see him on the ward. He couldn't recognize anyone or understand anything. I left. I went home. The flat was locked up. I rang the doorbells of the neighbours I knew. One neighbour opened the door. When she saw me, she slammed it in my face in sheer terror. Americans in American films never surrender. The hero fights the whole world on his own until he gets to the truth. I don't know how to do that so I accepted the embassy's offer to buy me a ticket to Moscow and here I am. So, what do you say?"

Psycho's intonation took on its professional wheedling tone as he said, "If we can be satisfied that we're not dealing with a displacement syndrome, split personality, or practical joke…, then

you need to find the money, go to Paris, and investigate."

"Here's the obituary. There's a photo." Iris handed Psycho a cutting.

"Does it look like you? It's just a newspaper photo…"

Iris looked for herself.

"Are you serious? It isn't me or anything like me. But not long ago that photo was different – or else I was."

Psycho thought about it. Only recently, as he modestly welcomed in 2008, a year bearing the sign of infinity as the wags had observed, he had seen General Secretary Leonid Brezhnev's New Year greetings to the citizens of the Soviet Union on YouTube. He had been struck by the fact that in 1981, a year before he died, Brezhnev looked like a doddery old man. He had looked the same in 1971 and indeed always. At the time, those same wags (Russia's most active social stratum) had joked: "I'm no fading star, I'm a superstar". And now there was this same Lyolik, looking, as they all did, to be in beetle-browed middle age. His hectoring victory speech was like one of Putin's. There were human touches to Gorbachev's and Yeltsin's (which Psycho watched next), i.e. an acknowledgement and sense of weakness rather than omnipotence and omni-control. Along the lines of "last year … problems … went wrong" whereas Lyolik and Who-is-Mr.-Putin were Kabuki theatre, which predicted robots long ago and had its actors mimic them even before they were invented.

Psycho simply couldn't process this feeling: at different ages and at different times, the world is different. Thirty years later, Lyolik, old and senile, was depicted by actor Sergey Shakurov, whereas the old clip on YouTube showed a Kabuki actor playing the petty Russian bureaucrat robot who was supposed to be the apex of the Russian pyramid. It had to weigh more than the rest of the structure put together in order to grind it into the ground. Otherwise, it would spread like weeds in all directions, shapeless and senseless, and drive everyone out of their minds.

These thoughts took no more than a second to flash across the screen of Psycho's brain. He didn't lose the thread of his conversation with Iris but he didn't know what to do with it. It was a self-weaving web. Convoluted nests of case histories were forcing her out as illegitimate.

"Still, you need to clear things up. Go to Paris," Psycho said again, clearing his throat as if his thoughts had sullied it.

"No. That's enough."

"I'm talking about your parents not… You need to find out about them. That's where it comes from, from your childhood. That's the only reason you planned to marry a Frenchman from what I remember."

But Iris now wanted to live for today: to draw a line and start from scratch, to be born again as an adult. She flicked through the diary, hoping to find something in the past to get some purchase on. She came across an entry on Sylvaine Personne. "That's so I can say 'That Sylvaine's me' and be off to the nuthouse again," Iris seethed at herself. "Why is it so clear and easy for other people? Father, mother, place of birth, school, work, residence. The classical unities of place and action. Unity of person wasn't even discussed. Then the places separated and diffused and action too: live as you please, without convention and ritual, swan around by aeroplane: you're an individual. Neoclassicism brought unity of person. That too is falling apart to embrace the whole world. That and that alone must be clasped tight lest an identity crisis leads to a crisis of the whole of civilization. In post-modernism, pretence is allowed: all the world's a stage and everyone's a player." Iris wasn't pretending. But could it be that holes had been made in the partitions dividing one personality from the next and a substance of some kind, which constituted the essential self, was bleeding through these wormholes and since it all was all taking place underground, beneath the earth, what was happening couldn't be understood on the surface and it was best to pretend that nothing at all was going on?

Iris rented the flat right opposite mine but I only got to know her through my upstairs neighbour, Natasha. I've known Natasha since our teens. She has a hard life – her husband's an alcoholic. As their daughter grew up, she started nagging Natasha. "You've got no self-respect if you won't divorce an alcoholic. I want nothing to do with a father like that." Natasha did make timid attempts to leave her husband but they tended to be ultimatums along the lines of "Stop drinking or I'm leaving." But she had nowhere to go. Her husband, my long-term neighbour, had brought her in from the provinces. All she could do was head homewards and neither party wanted to exchange their little flat for something even smaller. There was a time when Natasha was hatching plans to flee to Europe and begin a new life in a new place but the topic gradually dried up. Her daughter left home when she was a student and still has no desire to get married. Natasha's husband would get to the point at which he couldn't cope, would undergo hypnosis, swear off the drink, and pull himself together, but it never lasted long. Natasha would go crazy, cry, and poison herself popping pills, but she remained a devoted wife. That's how I've known her all my life: either tear-stained and haunted or glowing with the conviction that her husband is off the bottle for good. She's a dark-eyed, skinny little thing – not slim and shapely but skinny, and she doesn't have the dark eyes of the old song but rather something like the deep-set beads of a hedgehog. And yet Natasha doesn't elicit tears of tenderness or sympathy. She might be a bundle of nerves but she's a bundle of muscle too, ever ready to repel an attack. She radiates the courage to live through the cannots. To an outside observer, she's performed no heroic deeds but there's an air of heroic endurance about her and her eyes fling darts.

She pops in to see me in a state of agitation. "Guess what? He's pissed. Like I care. I'm happy. Does that surprise you?"

I watch and the black beads are wider apart as if only drawn close until then by sheer force of will, gathered together so that her gaze could lash out.

"D'you know what just happened? I come into the lobby and there's this young woman next to the lift. She turns round to look at me and as if she's seen a ghost, she just breathes, 'Natasha…'

"'Yes,' I say, 'I'm Natasha. Who are you?' I say because I don't know her face.

"'Iris,' she says. And then something did seem familiar. Iris isn't a name though and yet I feel like I've come across it before. She said she was a new neighbour, just temporary. She's replaced those people who went abroad, the ones who lived opposite you."

"I didn't think there was anyone there," I say to keep the conversation going. I don't know any of the neighbours at all, apart from Natasha, and that's only because she's super-sociable, always dropping in to apologize for the bath leaking into my flat, for the yells and the noise, the flower pots thrown onto my balcony – for her drunk of a husband, basically. At the same time, she provides me with a chronicle of their family life and so I know about her acts of heroism, his falls, their storm-tossed boat that will never smash against real life since real life is what it's made of.

"This Iris invites me round, gives me tea, and really looks me over. As if I'm the spitting image of some Natasha from Paris. That Natasha, the one just like me, escaped from her – and our – misery, got married to a nice French guy, and was enjoying life, and then she up and died in a car crash. Her son died too and her husband went crazy. The point of the story is that if I had left that drunk of mine and gone off somewhere, like I was planning to once, remember, the same thing would have happened to me. And she's certain of this because that Natasha wasn't just a friend. I don't really know what she was but she knew her as well as she her own self. So I've been lucky."

I was only half listening as I did to all Natasha's stories but it was nice to see her happy. I met the new neighbour, Iris, on the stairs and then she dropped in and I began eagerly devouring her tales of karma. I was a bit of a hermit just then. Not that I'd gone to live off roots in the forest. I was living among people but everything I had once wanted to be inspired by had either disappointed me or simply become part of me. I had developed an unexpected passion for collecting: people began to interest me per se, as bearers of fate. I looked closely, took note, and stored it all away for safe keeping. Before, other people had been a means of fulfilling my own desires and I was dependent upon them. Being a recluse means reducing your appetites to the bare minimum, curbing the self, becoming Nothing, an instrument that receives and makes records in some layer of the brain. I suggested that Iris and I went to see a clairvoyant I happened to know.

CHAPTER 10: IZABELLA

Izabella, who is either Spanish or Georgian, lives in a little house in outside Moscow that is visited by seekers from all over, who patiently wait their turn. I got to know her when I was a student and fascinated by parapsychology. I used to go to secret gatherings and listen, rapt, to tales of telekinesis, teleportation, and telepathy but it was clairvoyance that captivated me. How can you know something you don't know? It's a question of how knowledge is conveyed. If you see something when you're awake, read it or hear it on the radio, that's knowledge, whereas a dream or fantasy really isn't. A clairvoyant doesn't read minds but sees pictures from the past, present, and future – a future that doesn't yet exist. I'd read everything I could about the subject but had never met any clairvoyants. At one group, I was told about Iza from Sukhumi, whom I could visit but was not, under any circumstances, to tell that I was interested in the subject itself. Otherwise, she'd show me the door. Others had tried. I should pretend I'd come to discover my fate, listen to the prediction, hand over my ten roubles and only then ask questions.

And off I went, over the hills and far away, to Sukhumi. "If nothing comes of it, I'll get a holiday by the sea," I thought and then there were the cypress trees, the *khachapuri*, the scorching south, of which, as it turned out, there is never enough in life. But it was Iza who was the aim of the trip.

It was afternoon when I arrived at the marine club she managed but there was no-one there. I decided to wait a bit and in the meantime I examined the agitprop on the walls. Suddenly, I heard steps and at the same time a voice behind me. It took me only a few seconds to realize I was the topic of conversation. It was Iza. She didn't say hello. She didn't even glance in my direction. She went over to the table, which was covered in newspapers and magazines, and, shuffling them mechanically, talked as if she were speaking to herself. There were scenes from my childhood and adolescence, my father, mother, and home, and then she reached the present day. At the time, I wanted two things: to leave the husband I'd managed to acquire by then and to become a parapsychologist.

Iza said disapprovingly, "You're planning to leave your husband. Don't do it or you'll spend the rest of your life going from one to another. You will suffer. You'd be better putting up with it."

I'm sure I blushed. My plan was coming to a head but I was ashamed of it. Later, I would envy myself an innocence that didn't need marital vows to be ashamed of being bent on destruction. Iza was right: later on the energy produced by fission would be at work within me in spite of myself. I would want to break free regardless and would do so with ever-increasing ease.

Iza said, "What you think you'll turn into a career isn't going to happen. Your destiny hasn't started yet. It will start when you're twenty-three."

Since I considered myself an adult, I took umbrage at this and chose to end this trip into the future right there and then. I merely asked whether there was going to be war since at the time (in 1976) there were rumours that war with China was on the cards.

"No," she replied, "there won't be a war but in ten years' time there will be something like a revolution."

"Right," I thought to myself, "Iza may be able to see the past as clear as day but I'm not so sure about her version of the future."

Later, I had to admit that Iza had seen into the future, the real one, the one that actually happened. But then, to bring the session to a close, I offered her the ten roubles but she turned them down.

"That's not what you're here for. So, what do you want to know?"

We started talking. Iza didn't know why she had the sight or where it came from. Basically, she was an uneducated country woman although she held herself imperiously and with dignity, like a queen. I asked the usual dumb questions: did she see pictures or scenes, were visions of the past different from visions of the future, did she see everything all the time or not everything and not all the time…?

Her answer was to say, "Come and see me at home on the day I receive visitors. Sit and watch and draw your own conclusions."

I don't know why Iza was so well-disposed towards me. I spent the whole day at her house. Just as she had previously gone through the newspapers, now she chopped endless vegetables. Evidently, in order to see the invisible, she had to keep her hands busy. People came in one by one. They were from various places and she would say something to each one that caught their interest even though they hadn't asked a thing. One person had had something stolen. Another was suffering the pangs of love. Add in children and illnesses and that was it, all the issues. There was just one young woman she immediately tried to get rid of, calling her every name under the sun.

"I can explain everything," the woman entreated but Iza was relentless.

From the sidelines, it was difficult to tell what was going on, but they both knew and had a real set-to. The woman had done something nasty and Iza didn't want to forgive her or help her. Like a priest who either does or does not grant absolution.

"It serves you right," Iza concluded, menacingly, putting her out just as she was, in floods of tears. The clairvoyant is the real priest of our times – the all-seeing eye.

Soon after visiting Iza, I gave up the notion of studying parapsychology. The subject itself was closed to me. Physicists and mathematicians might find the key to time but not lyricists like myself. And I had definitely become a lyricist. At the age of twenty-three. I went to see Iza again but by then Abkhazia with its cypress trees and *khachapuri* had become a firing range. For Iza as a Georgian, the most obvious thing would have been to leave for somewhere peaceful in Georgia but, all of a sudden, she announced that she was Spanish and made her way to the Moscow area. There she set up a house and garden just like the ones she'd had in Sukhumi, although apples grew instead of tangerines, and plums instead of feijoa. She said she was Spanish and, as if by way of confirmation, told tales of Christopher Columbus - she'd probably seen the Ridley Scott film, the one with music by Vangelis.

We were drinking tea on the veranda. Iza, old now at nearly 70 but resolute as ever, Iris, jumpy and attentive, and myself, tired and distracted. We'd brought along a cake, Iza fetched some walnut preserve, and we chatted about the cold summer, recalled the cold winter, and consoled ourselves with the fact that, as a result of global warming, everywhere was getting colder. Iris began to talk about Natasha. Iza left the table and took us into the garden. She sat on a little, low bench and began to run her rosary through her fingers. Her movements were less rapid than before and she had begun to talk slowly and with effort.

"Iris has been left here from the future. Ten years from now, it will all become clear. People are being invented. People who have naturally grown out of a past like a rose from a bud are becoming fewer and fewer. Tanya now, she's real. You can't always tell who's from where. I'm old now. You're looking for the beginning, for Rosa's parents."

"Rosa?" Iris leapt up.

"That's right, Rosa. But I'm from the twentieth century, the century of electricity – the iron, the fridge – it's not for me to understand. I may cultivate these roses here but I wouldn't say they're my children and I have so very many of them even though it's all one plant." Isa got up, washed her hands at the outside tap, and began to show us her garden. Irises, peonies, golden balls, beds of courgettes and carrots.

Irises – velvety, claret-coloured irises, with yellow centres, violet, lilac. How odd to describe a colour by referring to Bordeaux wine, lilac, and violets. Black is the strongest colour. It blocks everything out, covers it up. You can't change black into anything else. You can't make it white or red. Iza always wears black. The colour of widowhood, the convent, renunciation. And of silhouettes. I also wear black a lot although I don't know the most important things about it: where photons go at night, the levels to which the speed of light falls when there is no light, or what non-light i.e. blackness is. I ask Iris and she replies that when she was a child she could see in the dark but can't see a blind thing nowadays.

She goes on to say, "Perhaps, Iza really could see the invisible once but can't see a blind thing now either."

"After all, seeing in the dark is another way of seeing the invisible," I think, looking out of the window of the train taking us back from Iza's. "Space is a darkness in which just a few small fires burn: the Sun that is ours and the stars that are not. Am I real? What did Iza mean?' I start daydreaming. 'Evolution is the evolution of creation. It took man as creator a lot of time to come up with the loom, to discover cotton in cotton bolls, or divine the silk in silk moths, the electricity in metal wire, or the computers in binary code. First he built a robot-bug, then a little dog. He still hasn't managed an artificial person. Perhaps our own Creator had many goes at things: there was paramecium-caudatum, a fish in water, a tiny burrowing creature, a dinosaur dragon, a monkey, a Neanderthal, a Cro-Magnon man and, finally, us. A long way from the peak of perfection but still we're the only creatures that are improving, not internally but in terms of the outer vessel. We are moving towards being able to write ourselves into other vessels, to detach the essential self from ourselves. Just as it was possible to detach the word from the body, from the vocal cords: to write on clay tablets, papyrus, and paper, to print using linotype, or to key into a computer. The word may be written on nothing at all – on a monitor screen or in the air – but it remains the same word that was scratched onto vellum with a goose-feather quill."

"Clairvoyance is a lie," says Iris, aggrieved.

"Clairvoyance is inside information," I think, "which is why it's denied and condemned."

CHAPTER 11: ROSA

In the autumn of 2004, not long before she returned to the waking world, Rosa was sleeping in my Very Good Friends' living room. They were entertaining guests from the upper echelons of the state. Conversation revolved around the subject of Russian fascism.

"Of course, you realize that Fascism of one kind or another is inevitable, just as it was in Germany after the collapse of the empire and defeat in World War I. The only protection is to simulate Fascism from the top down. That's exactly why we've set up a fascistoid party, with our own people acting as xenophobes. It will draw in the young yobs and gradually civilize them. After all, the yobs have energy to burn and we'll give it a peaceful outlet and extinguish it. Don't worry. Everything's under control."

Rosa sighed. Everyone turned round and stopped talking. The sudden sigh could be heard above the clamour of conversation.

"Being a queen is not the same as being a lady-in-waiting or a commoner. My every day is a struggle, my every step a risk. I won myself the title Queen of Castile. Otherwise, I would have remained simply the wife of Ferdinand of Aragon. It wasn't easy persuading him to accept equal rule – he was prepared to dissolve our marriage and then I would have lost everything. Dislodging Juana, whom my late brother Henry IV had declared heir to the throne of Castile, seemed an altogether impossible task. But I had the only idea likely to work: starting a rumour that Henry was impotent and Juana not of his bloodline. Such things had never before been spoken of in public and the court decided that so shocking a statement could only be the truth. Now, behind her convent walls, Juana can yell as much as she likes that she's the true queen of Castile: no-one can hear her voice. Having a voice that can be heard matters more than any written laws. The Vatican responds to my voice since I am building a truly Catholic realm. Following in the footsteps of the King of France, I established the inquisition. He eradicated a heresy and united some fine territories to France. I gave the Church free rein to judge all those of different faiths and to burn them at the stake. Protestants included. It is my desire to please the Catholic Church as other women desire to please a man. God has mercifully delivered me from beauty. All my subjects come to resemble me, as if they were my children, and what woman can boast of so many children and well-behaved ones to boot? This year, 1492, is a special one. I have reconquered Granada and dispatched the Moors to the very devil though they had ruled Andalucia for eight centuries. My forebears could not secure this victory for they lacked my clarity of purpose. Thus, they were unable to bring themselves to present the Moors with a single choice: leave or accept death. Ferdinand too rested his chin in his hands, ruminating, and so we would have continued between Scylla and Carybdis. Now Granada is our residence. We moved here on 6 January. Fortune is with me this year. No-one would ever have thought to move against the Jews. They have lived here always, they control the finances, many of them belong to high society, but I simply made them an offer: either accept the true faith or leave Castile or, rather, our new country of Spain. I brought about the deportation (I've used the Latin word for persuasion's sake) of hundreds of thousands of Sephardim but tens of thousands chose death.

"The Catholic state of Castile now consists of Castile, Aragon, Valencia, Granada, Malaga, and Barcelona and we shall soon catch up and overtake Portugal. At this point, a man turns up, suddenly and, as it happens, from Portugal – a Genoan, Cristobal Colon. He's poor. He wants money provided and an expedition mounted, supposedly to open a passage to the Indies. But this is no Vasco da Gama! Just a failed seafarer who sailed the seven seas with the Portuguese navy and has already presented his adventure to the Portuguese court. They laughed at him and dubbed his plan a pipe dream. And so he has made his way to Castile where some of our merchants are willing to back him. Colon is seeking an audience with me. Let him come.

"He has red hair, sprinkled with grey. People here fear redheads and decline to support the endeavours of those whose hair sparkles with silver. He is, at least, a pious man. Colon is forty-one years old. The honours achieved by that age are the ones you take to the grave and he has achieved nothing for all his ambition. Tall and stately, with a strong face, where has he been vegetating all this time? Our wise men easily dismissed his claim that the Earth is round. They delivered their response: 'An Earth shaped like a sphere would form a sort of vast mountain before him, through which he could not sail with even the fairest wind.' And yet, so what? I'll take another chance. If Colon really does discover a new world for us, we win and so does he. I've set his reward as one eighth of the profits since he's putting up one eighth of the costs. He will secure a title, the rank of vice-president of the new territories, and his children will be aristos. Ferdinand carps. He finds change hard to stomach. For my part, I keep up the pressure and give no-one time to come to their senses.

If not, the rumblings of dissent would already have spilled over into revolt.

"Colon has brought glory to the crown and now the sun never sets on Spain: as it disappears below our horizon here, so it rises in the New World. We have conquered the world. There is just one problem: the coffers are empty. The upkeep of our grandees who are bringing the savages overseas to the Christian faith is too costly. Colon made a suggestion, to send prisoners overseas. It's a good thought. But the grandees' hatred of Colon is growing and by the hour not the day. They have already brought him back in chains. I ordered them removed but I cannot sacrifice my royal mission for him. I have to take other people into account. Cristobal doesn't understand this. He has written a will, insisting that he be buried on an island in the ocean rather than in Spanish soil. The continent he discovered has been named after Amerigo Vespucci. And, Juana, my daughter with Ferdinand, has been nicknamed "the Mad". She desired to please not the Pope but a king and loved not God but a man and went out of her mind."

Moving onto dessert, my Very Good Friends squabbled over the eternal Russian question: what mattered most - the good of the people or the good of the state? The state employees smirked: what mattered was the goal and the goal was either to conquer the world like Hitler or to get though the day and endure the night like us.

"A couple more years and we'll come out on top, I swear. The future belongs to us."

"It does?"

"Uh-huh. We've got agents there, tee-hee."

There is a bouquet of irises on the table.

"Irises always make me think of Van Gogh," someone says. "He might have lost the plot himself after he cut his ear off but his pictures are so colourful."

"For me, the iris is the coloured ring of the eye. To go into an office, you put your eye up against an aperture, your iris is identified, and you can go in."

"Iridology is said to be the most accurate method of diagnosis. We'll have to try it otherwise how will you know whether or not you've got some disease?"

"Life's the disease – a fatal, sexually-transmitted infection, as observed by the quick wits of the Russian people."

Rosa was sitting up on the bed, her eyes closed, but her head hung heavy in the air, and she lay back on the pillow. The flower of the iris is a fantastical intricacy: all silken tongues of violet, enfolding glints of sunlight.

CHAPTER 12:
MY VERY GOOD FRIENDS

My Very Good Friends are Lena and M. They're a bit on the secretive side. I don't mention their names too often because I know they shun publicity and areas outside the VIP zones they're taken to in sleek, chauffeur-driven cars. At one time Lena was the most famous girl in the world. Now she's all but forgotten like Katya and Samantha, the little girls who played the role of angels to make peace between Russia and America. And the closer the event, the more distant the memory. People will know more about a skull dug up out of centuries of soil strata from its DNA. Small-scale Rosetta stones bolster human brain power whereas life today comes crashing down like a waterfall. Are you really going to remember something that is swept away by a foaming torrent? Once upon a time, if people learnt something, they remembered it for ever but now, and this just goes to show the accuracy of Warhol's "famous-for-15-minutes" concept, they're simply catching butterflies, the flickering images of events, the whiffling passing-by of names. Nothing of yesterday's "cult" remains as if the cult itself were senseless and fleeting as a dream. Lena had been Russia's first beauty queen and her father a Kremlin spin-doctor and creative (an "ideologist" as it was called at the time). Lena almost knocked the then US President off his perch but now she's a woman of poise who works in consultancy, in other words, does virtually the same thing as her father but in the public arena. Whether or not anyone actually needs her services or whether it's just a title, I don't know.

Seven years ago she married M. Now he's a real dark horse. That is to say, he's an antique dealer but rather an odd one. Their palatial house in the country is visited by denizens of the Kremlin, as Lena sometimes lets slip when she's talking to me, and it appears he's the one they come to see, not her. Perhaps they all have an interest in antiques?

I used to be friendly with M. He had a fling with someone I was friends with at the time, Mila. I saw him a couple of times but had to listen to entire epics about him from Mila in the innocent days of our friendship. That's a good idea, incidentally, looking up Mila and reliving our youth. She's a political journalist nowadays. She'd be easy to find. I hadn't met M. since until we suddenly found ourselves at the same party. He and Lena were married by then and I'd been dragged along by Iris. He didn't remember me but Lena responded eagerly when Iris talked about her theory of human origins. She was writing a dissertation about reincarnation (or 'incarnations', as Lena corrected me every time) so she knew all the relevant theories. On this occasion, the talk turned to extra-terrestrials. One of the guests had mixed with the Dogon people in Mali and he expounded their legends of descending from aliens from the star Sirius. Suddenly Iris said: "That's what we are – aliens. We've been sent into exile on Earth from some other planetary paradise, whatever its name, for bad behaviour. We've been clapped in the irons of our bodies, in bio-sacks, in solitary confinement. We tap the walls between us to communicate and strive to annihilate one another because we don't think our imprisonment is fair. Our neighbours, sure – they're banged up for a reason and they dragged us in as well so we'd really like to smash the bastards' faces in – their real faces, the ones hidden in the bio-sacks. We're are monitored by jailers from Paradise. Although Earth's a prison island and we can't escape from our bio-sacks of our own accord, we're always trying to come up with something, to escape, to fly away. They mainly monitor the state of our bodies. If a sack is the worse for wear or broken, if it's been destroyed by evil-doers, the soul, that is the essential self, is released, and has to be stuffed into another sack. As a result, multiplication is an absolute law of prison behaviour. Everyone is serving different sentences. Some get away with a very brief life in the bio-sack. Others have to serve five or a hundred such 'life sentences' before they mend their ways. It all depends on whether the soul has become eternal and indestructible on its road to reform or whether it remains unrepentant. The length of sentence can therefore be reduced or extended. Those declared free and fit for celestial bliss are withdrawn. They are collected by spaceship since Earth's gravity is impassable to their pure essence, and if a released soul lingers too long in the prison atmosphere, it begins to affect the lives of the prisoners in such a way that they go mad and, instead of the fear and obedience required to reform, they develop delusions of freedom – undeserved freedom, that is. Someone will manage to peek out of their bio-sack and catch a glimpse of their fellows arriving. Moved by compassion, these fellows may make contact themselves. In theory, contact with freedom is not allowed: tainted souls must be kept in isolation so that Paradise remains free of pollution."

M. listened attentively, head lowered. Alternatively, perhaps he was just asleep. At least, he didn't utter a word until the very end of the party. When Iris stopped speaking, the guests began to rub or scratch the backs of their necks and, after a brief discussion, they came to the general conclusion that crackpot theories per head of population were definitely on the up. Nevertheless, they all subsequently went over to Iris and asked her something individually. I sat off to one side, holding my glass. Lena came and sat next to me. We chatted and immediately we just sort of clicked. But I'm not going to say which of the theories I was familiar with were of interest to her. Since then she's occasionally invited me out to the villa (I can't bring myself to call a house like that a dacha) and, whatever the tight-lipped M. might actually say, he gives the impression of being well-informed about everything under the sun. It was the same thirty years ago too. Mila was constantly nagging him to tell her his real name but discovered, hanging out with his friends, that everyone called him M. At that point she decided it must be Em. For Emmanuel or Emile but preferred to interpret it as M. for Magus. She believed he had magic power.

She and I met the Magus together at a party that was a gathering of telekinesis and telepathy practitioners and the people studying them. It was a kind of club that met in the flat of a sick woman who evidently found it entertaining or was hoping for a cure from some sorcerer who might pop in. And the Magus had turned up as well. He was striking, arresting, with a hypnotic gaze, and he immediately cast a spell upon Mila. These days, by contrast, he endeavours to pass unnoticed. Mila gave him her phone number but the Magus didn't ring. And then, one day, she went to the Botanical Garden to revise for an exam. She was sitting on a bench, chewing her pen (strange as it may seem, there were no computers at that time), underlining passages in pencil, and making notes in an exercise book. There was no-one around. And suddenly there along a path she sees the Magus coming towards her. She leaped up in surprise, dropping her books and papers, bent down to pick them up, taking her eyes off the Magus for a second, and when she looked again there was nobody there. She was at a loss to begin with because there was no way of turning off the path but then she decided it had been a vision, deliberately created by the Magus for her to see. She shoved all her exam equipment into her briefcase and ran home. The Magus rang that very day and suggested she went with him to visit a friend's dacha. "Just bring a friend." And so she took me along and proceeded to bash my brains with her wretched vision for a good long time.

Mila said that M. always carried a gun. He would even put it up on the dashboard for everyone to see. Not only did he have a car but he shopped at Beriozkas (special shops using the foreign currency Soviet citizens weren't allowed to have, to say nothing of weapons) and smoked Marlboros, and all the while he was a complete mystery. He never said anything about himself.

"Where did you study?"

"We've all learned through our education

Some few things…"

"Where were you born?"

"In a maternity hospital. What's with the crazy questions?"

But Mila just couldn't resist asking,

"And what do your parents do?"

"Does it really matter?"

Straightaway, she realized that it didn't, was covered in confusion, but went on to ask,

"Where do you work?"

Not working or at least not being registered at a place of work was a criminal offence at the time. He replied, "I'm in cinema – an usher."

That said, he lived like a film star and behaved like one too, arrogantly, and with a sense of his own superiority, but justifiably so as it happens. Then, at the dacha – and the dacha belonged to the son of a famous composer; he'd inherited it from his father – the Magus took out his gun, put a tangerine on top of the half-opened door into the garden, and fired from a distance of about ten metres. He hit his target. It frightened me a bit but Mila was thrilled to pieces, seeing that his friend couldn't hit the target and he could. Then he played some classical piece on the piano. Mila thought he was brilliant. He asked for a violin and played that as well, after which he began to recite verses of The Iliad off by heart, passionately, and at length. Mila was amazed that he could rattle off such great chunks by heart and she made no bones about saying so.

"Ah, well, I thought girls would appreciate the lightning fall of unconquerable Troy, the hexameter, or the heroic endeavours of Gnedich's translation, if the worst came to the worst."

"Did you learn it off by heart specially?" Mila was bursting with questions again since surely no-one would learn something off by heart unless they had to. The Magus took a book off a shelf and asked Mila to open it at any page. She did so and he glanced inside, gave the book back to Mila, and told her to follow the text which he then delivered with expression.

"Do you know the whole book by heart?" asked Mila, stunned.

"No. I remember everything I see."

Mila took another book off the shelf. The same thing happened. Mila didn't know there was such a thing as a "photographic memory" but I'd read about it somewhere since I read anything I could get my hands on from morning till night. The difference in what we did and didn't know in this instance was less crucial than the difference in our attitudes: she was in love while I was a mere bystander. For this reason I noticed that the Magus was forever showing off and that it was rather wearing. But every day

Mila would try to win me over. He had cured her of the flu. He arrived. She had a temperature of 38 and a runny nose. He left and it was 36.6 and she was utterly ecstatic. He didn't do anything. They just talked for an hour or so. He could guess what she was drawing. And there was I, always the sceptic, as regards the healing power of love and the fact that it didn't take a seer when it came to her artwork. "You've always got a bit of paper when we're talking. You draw all over it."

"But he said I'm going to be a journalist not an artist." Mila had no doubt that this was a prophecy. "He said I'm always asking other people questions, whereas an artist asks questions of herself and sometimes of the Architect of the Universe."

"The Architect?"

I remembered this today at my Very Good Friends'.

"Does the phrase 'the Architect of the Universe' mean anything to you?" I ask the Magus disingenuously.

"If you regard the Universe as a palace then it has an architect but if you think the yard's overgrown with weeds because of cross-pollination, the housing department plonked down the bench for the old folks, and the kids have trampled out somewhere to play football, then obviously no architects were involved."

"And in actual fact?"

"There are palaces and there are yards and that's all, in actual fact."

"Have you heard anything about Rosa by the way?" I ask, remembering the other topic that connects me to my Very Good Friends.

"Who's Rosa?"

The Magus pulled a face but I'd already told Lena she was called Rosa. Evidently, she hadn't thought it interesting enough to tell the Magus.

"That's what Tanya calls our sleeper."

"Ah, right. Rosa it is then. The Lord works in mysterious ways."

"It will be New Year in a week. It's a year since she woke up and it was summer when she disappeared."

"Do you need her?" the Magus asks stiffly.

"I'd just like to be sure everything's okay."

"Fine. I'll make enquiries."

"Poor kid," Lena sighs. "I can't imagine what it's like, sleeping your life away."

"It depends what you consider sleep," says the Magus with a yawn and looks at his watch. "I have to be up early tomorrow."

Lena and I stay where we are for another ten minutes after he's gone.

"M.'s an early riser," says Lena as if apologizing.

"What's his real name?" I ask.

"You won't tell anyone, will you? It's Samuel."

"So why all the secrecy? Why do you call him M. (I'd never mentioned Mila)?"

"He doesn't like the name. It's too Jewish, too unusual, too pompous, if you like. I only know it because I've seen his passport when we've been travelling together."

"And when you got married presumably."

"We're not married."

"Why not?"

"So there wouldn't be any arguments over property. He's got a daughter and so have I."

"I didn't think he had any children. Where is she?"

"I've never seen her. She's abroad somewhere. You know how secretive he is."

"Menelaus hiding the fact that he's Jewish?"

"You know he can't stand it when people ask him questions. I don't know what he's hiding but the difference between us is quite simple. My parents are just around the corner. I was born in Moscow. I've lived in the public eye, whereas he's collected his antiques all over the world. As you know yourself, that could land you in court in Soviet times. So he got used to being deliberately obscure. And his parents have been dead a long time."

"Has he never said who they were or where they lived?" For some reason, I resolved to ask Mila's long-ago question.

"Doctors, I think, out in the sticks, nothing special."

As Lena's chauffeur drove me home, I thought about the fact that no-one really knows anything. We believe what we're told, we're not really bothered, and we only take an interest when someone's hiding something. A secret is like the sign of a truth, sown into that secret as it might be into a sack. A secret is what goes beyond the boundaries of what has been agreed. We've agreed that the sky is blue although it's all the colours of the rainbow but the lens of the eye has a particular way of seeing. We've spent far too long reaching agreement that the eye is the test of truth to reject it now. Samuel really is an unusual name and a marker that immediately brings to mind the prophet or a Jew. The Magus is better. It's obviously a joke. M.'s good too. Everyone interprets it their own way.

CHAPTER 13: LYUDMILA

Lyudmila was due to write a review of the year for the December issue – a calendar of events with accompanying commentaries. It was a more or less technical task but for the umpteenth night Lyudmila was at the computer, glued to the real life detective story unfolding online. It was quite genuinely the biggest event of the year. Then suddenly, there was this short play. By one Shakespeare Too. What, like the Shakespeare? What a terrible insult to the great bard! But there was an easy explanation: the great plays weren't written by Shakespeare but attributed to him, so why not just keep on attributing? So what if he's long dead? Need that really prevent him assuming authorship at a distance? So then, not the Shakespeare but Shakespeare Too, his shade, the ghost of Hamlet's father.

It was just then that I turned up to see Lyudmila. She was in a real ferment and could only talk about two things – Litvinenko and Shakespeare.

She asked me who I thought might be hidden behind the second of these names.

"Well, there are various theories: Francis Bacon, Christopher Marlowe, the group Ilya Gililov came up with in his book. How should I know?"

"And who's behind the polonium poisoning?"

"Just as Shakespeare's contemporaries weren't aware that his name was only a front, a brand – and the guessing's gone on for four centuries – we don't know anything for certain, we just read what we're shown, and fume about it being crazy. But then, we live in a crazy world."

"If we read all the sources and compared them in a brainstorming session the truth would be revealed there and then," said Lyuda, full of enthusiasm. As she always is, incidentally.

"Let's read the play out loud," she said. "It's only short. Here we go:"

Shakespeare Too

POOR LAERTES
DRAMATIS PERSONAE
Polonius
A Guard
Count Che
A General
A Spin-Doctor
Second Spin-Doctor
Master of the Centre
Grandfather Tsar
Von Stierlitz
Laertes
Ophelia (Lyudmila)
Guildenstern and Rosencrantz
Hamlet
Horatio and guests (Montague, Capulet, Eirene, Lavinia, the Weasel). A Stranger
The audience at a news conference

Scene I

1996. The Guard's office. He and Polonius are having a drink.

Polonius: Now's not the time to settle scores. I'm here because our aims coincide.

Guard: My aim's to protect Grandfather.

Polonius: Exactly that.

Guard: The people are bad for Grandfather's health but you just keep on serving up elections. Our voters don't the choices elections involve. Do you know the dream of the ordinary Russian male? "Let me die in peace" – that's what he wants.

Polonius: They want to live not die! Albeit without making any effort. Unlike us ourselves, who slog from dawn till dusk.

Guard: Unlike ourselves, who exactly is that? Rogues like you?

Polonius: Your tribe's had its fair share of names as well: Oprichniki, Okhranka, the bloody KGB, and now the State Security Enterprise. That sounds reliable... civilized.

Guard: Oh, get lost! You're crap at jokes!

Polonius: But seriously, be grateful to Grandfather that everyone shows respect for the Centre nowadays. And you risk losing that in a single day.

Guard: Persuade Grandfather to call off the elections.

Polonius: It can't be done. We can no longer be a khanate, a feudal fortress, a slave-owning area, or a primitive communal tribe of savages.

Guard: It'll be a khan who wins the election all the same. The people want the Tatar-Mongol yoke, full stop. Or else a lot of money.

Polonius: Famously, there is no money.

Guard: D'you mean you've got no money? But you're a billionaire.

Polonius: I've earned it.

Guard: The fucking gallows, yes.

Exit Polonius, heading towards his old enemy, Count Che.

Scene 2
Count Che's Office.

Polonius: Weren't you expecting me? I've got good news.

Count Che: My newsfeed updates every 10 seconds and that's only the sordid, grisly, stomach-churning news. Alyuminiyevich and I had 150 opinion polls conducted. Grandfather's rating is two per cent.

Polonius: I know. And I know the Centre's position too. But I collect money from all seven banks.

Graf Che: The ones that run the country like the seven boyars? Ha, ha, ha!

Polonius: Precisely. At that time, power lay in troops, now it's in money. Shall we form an alliance, with me as generator and you as distributor?

Graf Che (with a smirk): An alliance with a scorpion? Risking a fatal kiss?

Polonius: That's enough. You're hardly a frog yourself. And insults are counterproductive. Everyone can always use a steadfast tin soldier, which means there's zero risk for you.

Count Che: We've no option. We'll take the risk.

Scene 3
The Tsar's bedchamber. He is propped up on his pillows, reading Tolkien. Enter Polonius, bent double, either bowing or because he has a bad back.

Grandfather Tsar (tearing himself away from his book). You see the thing is power in itself is evil. Even a good wizard who touches the ring of power will immediately do evil. He won't able to help himself.

Polonius: Yes, Your Excellency. I mean – No, Your Excellency. It takes money to do good, and we've got a hundred million dollars to ensure a positive election result.

Grandfather Tsar: And how much is the state budget?

Polonius: Two hundred million.

Grandfather Tsar: You want to throw half the budget away on elections?

Polonius: It's not the same money, Your Excellency. This is the capital of love for you and our country's future. Investments, so to speak. Shares. Seven men have bought shares in the future.

Grandfather Tsar: And the war in Chechnya? They said that would all be over in three days and I've heard nothing but Chechnya for three years now.

Polonius: Order the war stopped and we'll stop it.

Grandfather Tsar: You think everything's so simple!

Polonius: It is, Your Excellency. A reallocation of cash assets.

Grandfather Tsar: Leave me alone. I'm not well.

Polonius: We'll get you better.

Grandfather Tsar: I'm tired. And I have no sense of support. Everything I think of leads to an impasse or the abyss. Mordor.

Polonius: Just one last little bit to go. You weren't sleeping at night. You've had three heart attacks. Is that all going to go to waste now?

Grandfather Tsar: I used to have the strength but power put paid to all that. That's what I'm saying: power is evil.

Polonius: After the elections, you can take the whole four years off if you like. We'll do everything for you.

Grandfather Tsar (with a start): What do you mean "for" me?

Polonius: Well, we'll be at your service. Or be your hobbits, if you prefer. Stick with me and you'll be fine. Because I never take on hopeless ventures. And you know I always win.

Enter Count Che.

Grandfather Tsar (to the Count, sternly): It's not a good time. I'm in a meeting.

Count Che: I know. Polonius and I have decided to join forces. But before embarking on the project, Your Excellency, allow me to set certain conditions.

Grandfather Tsar: Of course. I hadn't even thought about it. Is it about positions?

Count Che: Those too. I'll be head of your administration and tomorrow you'll dismiss the Guard and all the security officials.

Polonius: And I'll take charge of them and stop the war. Once you've won, of course.

Count Che: Use your head, sirrah. With your appearance, your nationality, and the general attitude towards you?

Polonius: That's rich coming from you. Unlike some people, however, I'm a realist. And thick-skinned to boot. You can't hurt me. I don't blush or become livid with anger. Security will be headed by the universally beloved General. I'll be his deputy. At the moment, less than half the Centre and the Army are with us. That's a mistake and I'll put it right.

Grandfather Tsar: You're taking a lot on.

Polonius: I always have and so far I've hit the bull's eye every time.

A sudden pause. Grandfather Tsar and Count Che exchange glances as they each remember the same thing.

Count Che: Which is not to say someone's head.

Polonius: You can give up dropping hints. The investigators have no further questions for me.

Grandfather Tsar: I would have asked, even so.

Count Che: Fine. Let it go. There's plenty to do and not much time to do it in.

Grandfather Tsar: You go at a hell of a speed, both of you.

Count Che: Regular Schumachers, we are.

Grandfather Tsar: Okay, at least you've made your peace. Now, if only Orcs and hobbits could get along as well.

Scene 4

*Three days after the elections, Polonius, the General, and
Count Che enter the tsar's hospital ward.*

Polonius: Forgive us, Your Excellency, this has done your
health no good at all.

Grandfather Tsar (to Polonius and Count Che): Nonsense.
I'll get through it. And you've done really well, guys. It wasn't
particularly to my liking, of course, but I've got my strength back
and my hopes, and that's what matters. Success gives you wings.
What's going on now?

Count Che: You've got some paperwork to do. We've
brought it with us.

Grandfather Tsar: Okay, fine. Hand it over.

Count Che: This one's about my appointment, then there's
everybody in the administration, the prime ministers, the
ministers…

Polonius: And this is the General's appointment, and mine,
and all the security officers. You'll enjoy reading those. We'll
be back for your signature in an hour. Oh, and we've already
bought you a new heart.

Count Che: It's here in a sealed package. State of the art
technology. They'll put it in today.

The General: You'll be a different person.

Grandfather Tsar: Different? Why?

The General: Everything's changing at such a pace in Russia
that you have to hurry up and change too. Someone wants to
make mincemeat out of you, say, and you're already someone
else. They go over to that person and you're different again.

Grandfather Tsar: Whereas it would seem, General, that
you were born with such a deep voice. I hope you're a democrat?

The General: A general who's a democrat is like a Jew who
keeps reindeer.

Polonius (quietly, to the General): That's enough now,
come on. (To Grandfather Tsar): Your Excellency, the

General has a weakness for these sayings but he's definitely one of us.

The General: Yes, sir, Comrade Supreme Commander-in Chief! Permission to leave, sir?

Count Che: We're all going. We'll be back later, just the two of us. (To the General, closing the door). Boy, are you in urgent need of an image consultant.

The General: I'm not that way inclined.

Polonius: Now, now, children, don't squabble. (To Count Che): There's this person I need to transfer from St Petersburg to work with you. Can you make it all official?

Count Che: What's his name?

Polonius: Von Stierlitz.

Count Che: Von Stierlitz, fine. There's room for everyone.

Scene 5
Two years later. The Tsar's country residence.

Grandfather Tsar: Come in.

Hamlet: Good day, Grandfather Tsar.

Grandfather Tsar: It's not particularly good. And in all the world there's only one person I can speak to frankly, and that's you, Hamlet. Because you commune with higher powers.

Hamlet: I'm not the only one.

Grandfather Tsar: I haven't met any others. I'm surrounded by Orcs. Goblins. Evil wizards. I've just finished reading The Lord of the Rings. It's taken me two years.

Hamlet: Is there something you want to ask?

Grandfather Tsar: Indeed, there is, my boy. You're my only hope. I've been enslaved. The evil wizard, Saruman, has me in chains and my family ensnared in something to do with accounts and foreign mansions. He's threatening exposure and an almighty scandal. I submit to him in all things. I am under an enchantment.

There's someone else as well. He was all friendship too then suddenly it appears he's turned the treasury into a financial pyramid and it's about to come tumbling down. What can I do, Hamlet?

Hamlet: Let the Count act as sphinx at his own pyramids. I can't offer any comfort when it comes to Polonius. He's got tentacles everywhere, poisonous ones, too. He's an octopus and you're just one man, with no-one you can rely on.

Grandfather Tsar: So, the stars, the charts, the ghosts – whoever it is you confer with – they promise nothing good?

Hamlet: There's the Prosecutor. Make an ally of him. Have him announce that the high-profile murder case has been solved. That'll put Polonius behind bars and you can start to unravel the webs he's spun.

Grandfather Tsar: And what if Saruman ups and carries out his threats? Maybe I should put the frighteners on to start with?

Hamlet: If you just pick at a boil and don't have it removed, it only gets worse.

Grandfather Tsar: "Removed" – that covers a multitude of sins! You can remove someone from office, from a country, kill them or, as we say, "waste them". And of all of it's covered by "removed".

Hamlet: You'd do better not to dwell on that last meaning.

Grandfather Tsar: And tell me about Alyuminiyevich, too, Hamlet. Is he with the Count, with Saruman, or me?

Hamlet: How should I know? I can write down all your questions and ask, then bring you the answers.

Grandfather Tsar: That's you protecting your sources, but I'm still interested in this spiritualism of yours.

Hamlet: It's not spiritualism and I'm not protecting anything. It's just that you won't believe me in any case.

Grandfather Tsar: I do believe you. What you say is always to the point. It's just that today you're keeping me in the dark about something.

Hamlet: No, I'm not. Do you want to hear what they told me, word for word? I'll read it out right now. I took notes. "Grandfather Tsar has abdicated in favour of Von Stierlitz.

NB: Polonius–London–Laertes. Count Che remains at court."

Grandfather Tsar: Bollocks! Who is this Von Stierlitz? Just someone in my administration, on the lowest rung of the ladder. I'm abdicating? I'm not Nicholas II! Or are we about to have a revolution?

Hamlet: There was no mention of a revolution. And I certainly asked enough questions.

Grandfather Tsar: Who did you ask?

Hamlet: I have this friend. She lives in another time – in the future. You know about flying saucers, don't you? Well, basically, these people can fly here. Sometimes they manifest here too. That's how I met her. She's stunning. Ophelia, that's her name. She likes me too but she said she can't get involved or even talk about things that haven't happened here yet. Although for her it's the past and all her contemporaries know about it. When we're talking, everything just becomes clearer. Yesterday, I was so persuasive about the benefits of crib sheets, taking notes into exams, asking the audience, and phoning a friend that she just dictated these strange words.

Grandfather Tsar: You're having me on. What sort of science fiction is this, for crying out loud?

Hamlet: I knew you wouldn't believe me.

Grandfather Tsar: Fine. Can you bring this Ophelia here?

Hamlet: She'd love to see you in the flesh.

Grandfather Tsar: She's not an oracle or something, is she?

Hamlet: She's just an ordinary girl but from the future. Do you understand?

Grandfather Tsar: What's not to understand? The future's the future even in darkest Africa. Bring her to me.

Hamlet: It's just that Ophelia will choose the date and time.

Grandfather Tsar: Who is this girl to appoint a time for the tsar?

Hamlet: She's from the future. She can't always fly in. She has her own schedule there.

Grandfather Tsar: What, a more important one?

Hamlet: It's not about importance. It's not always technically possible.

Grandfather Tsar: I have meetings and engagements too. What am I supposed to say – sorry but I'm off to meet the future?

Hamlet: There's someone behind the curtain. (He grabs a tennis racquet off its peg and strikes the curtain. There's the sound of a falling body followed by rapid footsteps. Hamlet looks out and sees Polonius running towards a car, clutching his head.) It was a rat.

Grandfather Tsar: Time to set a trap. Off you go, my young friend, and bring the future back with you.

Exit Hamlet. Grandfather Tsar makes a phone call.

Grandfather Tsar (quietly, into the handset): Polonius has crossed the line.

Voice on the phone: The state line?

Grandfather Tsar: An unwritten line.

Voice on the phone: The one that really matters. (Pause) You want it sorted?

Grandfather Tsar: Turn him into a fish in a bowl.

Voice on the phone: Then grill him?

Grandfather Tsar: What a bloodthirsty nation! Put him in a goldfish bowl, all nice and civilized. Just keep the lid on tight.

Voice on the phone: Of the coffin?

Grandfather Tsar: Why on earth do Russians think their sense of humour is their best feature?

Voice on the phone: Sense of humour left behind, Your Excellency. It will all be done properly. We'll waste him in the bowl.

Grandfather Tsar: There you go again!

Scene 6
Rosencrantz and Guildenstern enter Polonius's residence.

Rosencrantz: The things we've learnt!

Polonius: I'd rather keep it specific: video, audio, photos.

Rosencrantz: Audio. Grandfather Tsar has decided to, you know, deal with you. These are the tapes. Here's the transcript.

Polonius: So, we put the screws on.

Rosencrantz: There's no point. Read the transcription. What's that bruise on your forehead, by the way?

Polonius: I don't need medical assistance from you. (To Guildenstern.) And what's up with you? Cat got your tongue?

Guildenstern: I'm the silent type. Means I don't blab either. (Looks at the bruise.)

Polonius: I've been wanting to ask for ages why you've got these Masonic nicknames.

Rosencrantz: Our organization's a secret one as well.

Polonius (scans several pages, drums his fingers on the table, bites a nail, kneads his forehead.) Get Laertes in here.

Rosencrantz: Laertes? What's he got to do with anything?

Guildenstern: Consider it done.

Polonius: I want him here tomorrow. Today, he'll be given an order to eliminate me. And wear masks. The other two as well.

Rosencrantz: Fancy dress?

Polonius: Yeah, like the Masons. Right, so, tomorrow at 1200, there'll be a news conference here. About the Centre's illegal order to assassinate a statesman.

Guildenstern: Need any security back-up?

Polonius: I don't, no. But in the meantime, keep tabs on Hamlet. 24/7. Audio, video, photos. (Rosenkrantz.) Laertes is yours.

Rosenkrantz: I still don't get it. Why Laertes?

Polonius: Understanding's not in your job description. Out!

Scene 7

Hamlet (on the phone): Grandfather Tsar, she's here, right next to me.

Grandfather Tsar: Who is? I'm watching a news conference on TV. The game's up, Hamlet.

Hamlet: I'll switch in on but Ophelia's flown in. She hasn't got much time because she has to visit the Armoury. That's the tour she's booked.

Grandfather Tsar: Hamlet, you're crazy. What effing Armoury? Polonius has won. I've lost. What do I want with Ophelia now? Can you hear it?

Hamlet: Yes, yes, it's on. I can see Laertes, people in masks. They've refused to kill Polonius. I nearly killed him myself with a racket. I'll talk to Ophelia and get back to you.

Grandfather Tsar: You come to me, here in the Kremlin. She can skip the Armoury, okay? I'll send an official car to get you.

Hamlet: It's okay. We'll make our own way there.

Grandfather Tsar: You can't get to the Kremlin by Metro!

Scene 8
Laertes and Polonius, seated.

Polonius: You saved my life. I'm in your debt. Whatever you want in life, come to me as if I were your father.

Laertes: I did what I considered my duty. The Centre shouldn't assassinate people. Otherwise, it's just a gang of criminals. But I won't survive whatever. They'll get me sooner or later.

Polonius: You will be under my protection. Today we won, and the country's in my hands, in mine and yours, Laertes!

Laertes: Is Grandfather Tsar of the same opinion?

Polonius: From tomorrow, I'll start looking for someone to replace him.

Laertes: What do you mean – replace him?

Polonius: In Russia, more than anywhere else, you have to keep up with the times. To start with, that Centre of yours must be headed by someone we trust. Then you'll have nothing to fear.

Laertes: You're talking as if…

Polonius: Tomorrow Grandfather Tsar will sign a decree making Von Stierlitz head of the Centre. He'll sign it like a good little boy. He won't even know who drew it up for him.

Scene 9

Enter Hamlet and Ophelia. Grandfather Tsar's Office.

Grandfather Tsar: So you're Ophelia. When were you born?

Ophelia: 1999.

Grandfather Tsar: So you haven't actually been born yet?

Ophelia: If I had, I wouldn't be able to fly in here.

Grandfather Tsar: Why?

Ophelia: There are restrictions. Our shades live among you – they're living shades, but they're not our real selves.

Grandfather Tsar: Whoah! What?

Ophelia: The soul can't be digitized. You don't know that yet. It's true that knowing doesn't help. Even knowing everything you know, I can't do anything to help.

Hamlet: You said you'd help.

Ophelia: I said I'd offer suggestions.

Grandfather Tsar *(feeling out of his depth.)* What is this? The Secrets of the Spanish Court?

Ophelia: The longer it goes on, the fewer choices there are. You only have one option left – quietly take your pension, don't get involved, and keep quiet as everything you achieved is destroyed day after day.

Grandfather Tsar: I have never surrendered.

Ophelia: Once upon a time, we all thought like that. You could chose death, humiliation, or jail, but you're not going to do that.

Grandfather Tsar: Tomorrow I'll make Polonius's sworn enemy prime minister. He'll beat him to a pulp.

Count Che at the door, dishevelled.

Grandfather Tsar: Che, what are you doing bursting in here? This is an important conversation.

Count Che: I wouldn't have, but nothing's more important than the news that's just come in. Default in Russia.

Grandfather Tsar: What's this new jargon?

Count Che: It means game over, collapse, finish. The money's gone.

Ophelia *(to Grandfather Tsar)*: Your fate is sealed and nothing will change it.

Count Che: You're a bold little madam. I can't quite seem to place you.

Ophelia: I'm just visiting.

Grandfather Tsar: Count, you sort out the finances. This is rather more important.

Count Che: Everything's determined by money.

Grandfather Tsar: Everything's determined by fate not money. And that you can't buy, understand?

Count Che *(aside)*: Polonius is right. He has lost his marbles.

Grandfather Tsar: What are you mumbling about? I'm sorry. I haven't introduced you. Hamlet, Ophelia, Count Che.

Ophelia: You'll always come back up to the surface.

Count Che: You can stop right there. To you, I'm also the person the whole country's allergic to.

Ophelia: To us, that's just a fantasy film. Not many people even know it.

Grandfather Tsar: How could I forget to ask what's happened to Russia in your time?

Ophelia: Drown'd, drown'd. No, no *(laughs)*, it's just a saying.

Count Che: Have I somehow come to the wrong place? Is this the Kremlin or the mad house? *(Exits with a dismissive gesture.)*

Grandfather Tsar *(smiling)*: As far as you and I are concerned, it doesn't matter anymore if it's the Kremlin or the mad house.

Ophelia (looks at her watch): The Armoury! (Blowing kisses, exits at a run.)

Hamlet: Well, there you have it. I'm in love with her, Grandfather Tsar, but there's no future in it.

Grandfather Tsar: After that conversation, I've stopped understanding what the future is. I'd stopped understanding even before that. There seemed to be a future in 1991. In 1998, my life was behind me and it hadn't been anything like I'd imagined.

Scene 10
Polonius's reception rooms. Enter Rosencrantz and Guildenstern.

Polonius: So, what have you dug up, mother fuckers?

Rosencrantz: Hamlet finds everything out from Ophelia. She's like a fortune teller but she's barking mad.

Polonius: Get her in here. Immediately.

Rosencrantz: We're not stupid, Mr. Polonius, sir. She's here already.

The door opens. Enter Laertes and Ophelia.

Laertes: Ophelia. Be gentle with her, Polonius, my friend. She's charming.

Polonius: Come now. Who are we working for then?

Ophelia: No-one. I'm travelling.

Polonius: For some reason, we find travellers tend not to get out of the Kremlin.

Ophelia: I want to find out what happened. The truth.

Polonius: Leave me and the young lady alone.

Exeunt all bar Polonius and Ophelia.

Polonius: I'm hoping you'll talk frankly now. Why are you acting the fool? What are you after in truth, seeing you brought it up?

Ophelia: Poor Laertes!

Polonius: Don't worry. He'll grow up a bit and become head of the Centre.

Ophelia: He won't.

Polonius: Now we're getting closer to the truth: are you clairvoyant?

Ophelia: It's best if I say yes.

Polonius: Excellent. Where's my wallet?

Ophelia: I don't know.

Polonius: There, you see, you can't even answer a simple question like that. Even a fool would have given an answer. How long has Grandfather got left as Tsar?

Ophelia: Everyone knows that. Until New Year's Eve, when they drink the New Year in. Whoops, I shouldn't have said that.

Polonius: ???

Ophelia: I'm not supposed to… mind you, what can be changed?

Polonius: When they're drinking in the New Year – it's a nice thought. There's a few months to go.

Ophelia: No, not now. In a year's time. Whoops, I've done it again. You must be hypnotizing me.

Polonius: You know, I rather like you, Gorgeous. Have dinner with me?

Ophelia: I've got to be going.

Polonius: What if Hamlet comes too? He is your boyfriend, isn't he?

Ophelia: I accept, just not today. On… hang on… on February 1, 1999. That will be my farewell visit.

Polonius: You little fuckwit! Ha, ha, ha! D'you think I'll have any recollection of you on February 1? If you only knew how many of your sort there are hanging around. Supermodels. A damn sight prettier than you and without bats in the belfry either.

Ophelia: There's something to do with you that's still not clear, so I'll be back for the answers.

Polonius: What is it you think I am, the prince of darkness or a stage villain? The journos all but wondering whether there's a better player than me in the country, if you think of the country as a computer game.

Ophelia: And do you know what game you're playing?

Polonius: I know more than you do. That's it. You're free to go. Laertes!

Enter Laertes, Rosencrantz, and Guildenstern.

Polonius: Take her to Hamlet. Where is he at the moment?

Rosencrantz: Celebrating Horatio's birthday.

Polonius: Laertes, you stay.

Exeunt others.

Ophelia (shouts back): Poor Laertes!

Scene 11
Horatio's flat. The door bell rings.

Horatio: Coming! (He opens the door to see Rosencrantz and Guildenstern.) Who do you want?

Rosencrantz: Happy birthday, Mr. Horatio! We'd like to talk to Hamlet.

Horatio: Hamlet, it's for you.

Hamlet (comes out): Hiya! I know your faces but I can't quite place you.

Rosencrantz: Rosencrantz and Guildenstern. We've been escorting Ms. Ophelia. We have an urgent message from her.

Hamlet: Are you from there too? (Points a finger upwards.)

Rosencrantz: Indeed.

Hamlet (calls to Horatio who has gone back inside): Horatio, shall I go outside or can they come in?

Horatio (coming back): Any friend of yours is a friend of mine. Please. The party's in full swing. Come in. Introduce them to the guests, Hamlet.

Hamlet: Friends of my beloved.

The General: I don't know who your girlfriend is but this pair are Rosencrantz and Guildenstern, Polonius's henchmen.

Hamlet (to Rosencrantz and Guildenstern, sternly): Is this true?

Guildenstern: We serve our country.

Rosencrantz: I told the truth. We were escorting Ophelia here to the party. She really did go to see Polonius and he ordered us to escort her but, on the way here, she disappeared.

Hamlet: What do you mean disappeared? What have you done to her?

Rosencrantz: We were in the car, talking. She goes, "Tell Horatio that it's because of him that we know our history." I go: "What history do you mean?" She goes: "Tell him just what I said." I go: "You can tell him yourself, Ms. Ophelia."

Guildenstern: I was in the passenger seat. I got out and opened the door for her.

Rosencrantz: I was sitting next to her in the back. I got out and walked round to her side.

Guildenstern: When I opened the door, she wasn't in the car.

Rosencrantz: Or when I got there. But she was there when I got out.

The General: I'll put a call through. They'll find her.

Hamlet: There's no need. I know what's happened. Let's carry on with the party. Ophelia's safe.

Montague: Under the current anti-people regime, being outside in the evenings is a like crossing a mine field.

Capulet: So do you advocate a concentration camp and constitutionals under the eye of prison guards?

Hamlet (under his breath): I can hear Ophelia's voice. It's like she's commenting on every line: "The General will die in a chopper, For Capulet tea does the deed. A bullet will go through Lavinia fired by the man who says 'Not what we need.' It's a poem. I'm going mad.

Montague: Not what we need, Capulet, you and your labels. As you know, there are two regimes in Russia: the cold which is bracing, although anyone who thinks it's the Cote d'Azur and wanders around half-dressed will freeze to death, and the thaw when everything's spead everywhere and everyone's up to their ears in shit.

Lavinia: We've shifted truckloads of shit but there weren't enough trucks. Never mind, we'll keep going with shovels and, don't you worry, Montague, we'll get round to you too.

A mobile phone rings.

Montague *(exits with his mobile, returns)*: General Lev's been murdered. We'll impeach Grandfather Tsar for this.

Hamlet: Why are you blaming it on Grandfather? It's Polonius's doing. And not for the first time.

The Weasel: Heads used to fly in every states when they were becoming established. Human rights were added on later. Well, one day Russia will become established too and be as soft as down. As for whether it's Polonius or not…

Capulet: Incidentally, Polonius has made my protégé, Von Stierlitz, head of the Centre. An excellent choice. As for Grandfather Tsar, I agree: we set out as brothers-in-arms but he's out to get me too these days.

Horatio: How strange that even the best-informed people, as present company would appear to be, don't know what's going on right under their noses. Who can know the truth then? No-one ever knows anything. Even if they're Nostradamus himself.

Lavinia: Keep on writing, keep on writing, it will count in your favour, Horatio.

Hamlet: "Horatio will remain in this hell. He must be witness to a nightmare. Eirene will be shot on the wing and the Weasel's fur will be flayed off him in jail."

Eirene: Hamlet, what's wrong? You keep muttering under your breath.

Horatio: Under their noses, under his breath – that's funny. Really, though, Hamlet, you're not yourself. Are you worried about Ophelia?

Hamlet: If I'm worried about anything, it's my sanity.

Eirene: I have a question, by the way. Why is it, Hamlet, that you're Grandfather Tsar's confidant?

Hamlet: He just has confidence in me.

Eirene: That's what so strange. That he should have confidence in someone whose mind is disturbed. Pardon my bluntness.

Hamlet: Most likely, a damaged instrument in a damaged country is more convincing. (To Rosencrantz and Guildenstern.) How come you're as quiet as mice? Play something on the guitar. (Produces a guitar.) You don't mind, do you, Horatio, my friend, if these rosy-cheeked twins play your famous strings?

Rosencrantz: We can't play the guitar.

Hamlet: Oh, really? You can manage to jangle my nerves but not a mere seven strings!

Rosencrantz: We haven't said a thing to you, Mr. Hamlet.

Hamlet: You're spies for Polonius and you're here to record everything we say. You've a video camera in one button (he rips it off) and a voice recorder in the other (he rips that off too).

Guildenstern: Do something! Stop him!

The Weasel: It's what I always say, such savagery, even at a friendly get-together.

Montague: It's nothing new to me. Grandfather Tsar's not right in the head so all his spawn are just the same.

Lavina: You're right to say they're spies, Hamlet, but not to rip their buttons off.

The General: If the mission is to find spy equipment, I'll find it.

Capulet: There's no such mission. Just calm down, all of you. You've had too much to drink and you're making a din. The doctors have told me I should only drink tea. Like the old Vysotsky song: "No, thank you, brother democrats, just tea."

Horatio: Everyone's forgotten it's my birthday.

Guests (all together): Happy birthday to you-ou-ou!

Horatio: Thank you. I'm touched.

Hamlet: Where've they gone?

The Weasel: Those spies of yours? To sew their buttons back on. (Loudly) I'm gonna fuck off out of here… I suggest you all do the same.

Hamlet: Weasel fur is the most valuable of all.

Scene 12
1 February 1999. Laertes's empty office.

Polonius: He's such a bastard. He virtually called me a murderer on TV. The case is solved, he said. The three of them cooked it up – Grandfather Tsar, that blasted Prime Minister, and his puppet of a prosecutor. There'll be prison van here for me tomorrow.

Von Stierlitz: Who are you telling this to? I'm right here.

Polonius: Realistically, how can you stop them?

Von Stierlitz: Elementary, my dear Watson. All white and fluffy doesn't really work here. You can't tell it from the snow. Every single one of them's as black as night and no amount of washing will make them white, although the Prosecutor spends enough time in the bath-house and with women too.

Polonius: Was it Rosencrantz and Guildenstern who made the recordings?

Von Stierlitz: Why do you care who it was? Here's the tape. We'll put it on TV tonight. He'll resign and that's all there is to it.

Polonius: And the Prime Minister?

Von Stierlitz: What about him? One thing at a time. We parry the blow when the sword's raised against us. We'll make pre-emptive moves later. We're not tsars yet.

Polonius: I swear on my mother's life, I'll make you tsar. I've only just realized: you've got to be tsar.

Von Stierlitz: There you go. Your eyes lit up at that. The most important thing for you is to come up with a project. Then you come alive.

Polonius: It's time we went our separate ways. We mustn't be seen together.

Von Stierlitz: We're in Laertes's office. He's been sacked, which means we're invisible. I'll go out through the door. I don't need to hide. And you can take the secret passage straight back to the Masons.

Polonius: What joker came up with those nicknames? For goodness sake: Guild Star and Rose Cross!

Von Stierlitz: Cross is "Kreuz" in German.

Polonius: It must be Danish then. The way that Denmark's a prison.

Von Stierlitz: "Then is the world one." But that won't stop us.

Scene 13
Hamlet and Ophelia, seated, on a sofa.

Hamlet: What a sad day! I'll never see you again. Just like the rock opera.

Ophelia: We could have stayed together. It's hard to explain but I'll try. I live in 2005. That's not what we call it but at least you get the idea. And we can make copies of ourselves and send them back into the past. The copy doesn't remember where he's come from and can't go any further than the time in which the copy was made.

Hamlet: Is it like copying a DVD?

Ophelia: A bit but without the DVD. Coming here's risky for me but I just had to know what really happened. In order to do so, I have to go back and be myself for ever. When you make a copy of yourself, you produce different versions so your memory is destroyed too. Basically, if I stay here I won't remember anything. And I won't know who you are. I can give the copy a name, though.

Hamlet: Your name? Then I'll find you straight way. We don't have names like that.

Ophelia: Not my own, I can't. I suggest Lyudmila. That contains three personalities all at the same time: Lyusya, Lyuda, and Mila. It will be more interesting that way.

Hamlet: It's as if I can understand the words you use but I can't grasp the meaning. What if I go with you and we live in your time without any copies?

Ophelia *(laughing)*: No. You'd need something you don't have in order to come with me.

Hamlet: What is it? Brains? Money? Will I be too old in the future?

Ophelia: I never even thought about you being older once you reached our time. Not many people will live that long, Hamlet. Perhaps it's better that way.

Hamlet: Surely you can tell me something about your life? Whether you clean your teeth, what toothpaste you use? Whether you walk to work and what you do? Is there peace or war? Come on. Surely it isn't such a deep, dark secret?

Ophelia: It's unauthorized advertising. *(Laughs.)* The history of civilization is officially at an end. *(Hums a fanfare.)* And that's all I'm telling you.

Hamlet: Well, you don't seem to be made of metal so what is it that's actually ended?

Guildenstern and Rosencrantz, in a car, recording the conversation.

Rosencrantz: Why are we recording this crap?

Guildenstern: We were told to record it and that's what we're doing. Ophelia's crazy. She runs away from the mental hospital to see Hamlet. Sure, we haven't caught her in the act. She's an expert in shaking off whoever's tailing her.

Rosencrantz: The boy's completely lost his head. Grandfather Tsar's been sidelined, Ophelia's here one minute, gone the next, stringing him along, messing with his head. Tell you what, mate, we've been lucky with our own girls, nice and quiet, no fuss.

Guildenstern: It's high time the stupid git got married. I just don't understand why he surrendered to Polonius.

Rosencrantz: Like it matters to us. We were told to make recordings. We're doing it.

Guildernstern: And if we're told to waste him?

Rosencrantz: We're not hired killers. We're a bit better than that.

Guildenstern: Laertes is wandering around without a job. He's not an assassin either.

Rosencrantz: He's got it made. Polonius has adopted him.

Guildenstern: Did you hear what she just said?

Rosencrantz: I've had it with the lovey-dovey stuff.

Guildenstern *(guffaws)*: I don't believe it. He goes: "When can I expect a copy of you." And she goes: "It's hard to say." Basically, she told him where to get off.

Rosencrantz: Why do we care?

Ophelia: What time is it? Polonius invited us to dinner last time I saw him.

Hamlet: Are you taking the mickey? As if I'd have dinner with Polonius!

Ophelia: You have in the past.

Hamlet: In Russia, everything changes very quickly. Yesterday's hero becomes a criminal, your friend becomes your enemy, and vice versa. You can't take your eye off what's happening for even a day although you'd really like to fly off somewhere. Perhaps you've got a different globe?

Scene 14

August 1999. Polonius's reception rooms and busy election headquarters.

Polonius: That's a major achievement: Von Stierlitz is Prime Minister, but we're not even half-way to achieving our goal.

Spin-doctor: True. Von Stierlitz's rating is zero and time's running out. There are no other options: introduce the post of deputy PM, then force majeure, power automatically transferred, and parliamentary elections deferred for a year. We'll do what needs to be done after that.

Polonius: Any other views?

Second Spin-doctor: We won't get away with the deputy idea. What we need to do is buy the biggest party in parliament and get them to nominate someone.

Polonius: Are you sure you not really fantasy writers? Perhaps you'd also like to suggest that extra-terrestrials kidnap our rivals?

Spin-doctor *(offended)*: If there's kidnapping to be done, we've got the Chechens. Or they could just come a cropper.

Polonius: The people are out of control. They're a law unto themselves.

Or had you forgotten?

Second Spin-doctor: The election results can be chosen at random.

Polonius: Honestly, what a land of fools! Isn't there a single person who can think properly? They're either too Soviet or out and out mobsters.

Spin-doctor: If you don't need my services any more, then I've got masses of offers.

Polonius: Leave them for now and listen to me. Here's what you have to do. First: You set up a new political party. I want the blueprint on my desk one week from now. The party itself will be fully formed in two months' time because in three months' time, it's the elections.

Second Spin-doctor: The blueprint's no problem.

Polonius: So get on with it.

Spin-doctor: As for who's in the party – three popular figures and a crowd of extras?

Polonius: You're on the right lines, Comrades. Go and summon the Master of the Centre.

The Spin-doctors go over to the other members of the election staff who are engaged in a discussion. What they say is inaudible.

The Master: Roll up, roll up – special operations! Reductions for loyal customers. Place your orders now.

Polonius: I have an order.

The Master: Chops, shoulder, bull's eyes?

Polonius: I seem to be hearing a lot about bull's eyes just now for some reason.

We're going to put some serious events in motion. Von Stierlitz has to become Ilya Muromets and Chapayev, hero and saviour. Any preparations in hand?

The Master: We've got entire units just standing around. Books of projects no-one needs that are gathering dust. Our best minds are on the verge of going soft.

Polonius: You've won markets with those minds. But our mission's secret and mustn't be revealed under any circumstances. Leave any traces and they'll be your traces.

The Master: Clear as crystal, Comrade Polonius. Now, about the budget?

Polonius: If anyone in this country ever asks what needs doing before they ask about money, I'll erect a solid gold monument in their honour.

The Master: It wouldn't last for five minutes if it was made of gold.

Polonius: How long has Iron Felix stood out there? A golden monument would be there just as long. Fear stops even theft in this country. Stir up as much fear as possible. Not a damn thing gets done without it.

The Master: Yes, sir, Comrade Polonius. We'll stir up shed loads of it. *(Exits.)*

Scene 15
2005. Horatio's birthday.

Horatio: That's it. I'm not expecting anyone else. This is Hamlet, an old friend, and Lyudmila, my niece, who's a journalist.

Hamlet *(launches himself at her)*: Ophelia!

Lyudmila *(steps back)*: Hamlet surely sees Ophelia everywhere. I'm Lyudmila. I expect you've read my articles.

Hamlet: It's ages since I read a newspaper. There's no point if you're out of work.

Horatio: That's only temporary. You'll always find something to do.

Hamlet: There's nothing more permanent than something that's temporary. Every year, fewer and fewer people come to your birthday parties. And that's permanent. Not temporary.

Horatio: At one of them, Capulet said he was only drinking tea. The way he said it made it stick in my mind. A couple of years later he drank a cup of tea and wham!

Hamlet: The tea was poisoned.

Horatio: That's just a guess. History is made up of falsified facts. So be careful what you write.

Lyudmila: It's not worth writing in case you get poisoned too.

Horatio: I'm writing my own "History of the Russian State" for the future. The truth and nothing but the truth. So that won't be published any time soon.

Lyudmila: Twenty years from now maybe, in 2025?

Hamlet: 2025! Ophelia!

Lyudmila *(contemptuously)*: Yes…

Hamlet: Yes?

Lyudmila: Horatio, please tell this friend of yours to cut the comedy. You and your Ophelia! You're as clingy as a limpet. Carry on with your reminiscences instead. I'll listen and then get them published in the paper. Ha, ha.

Hamlet: Rosencrantz and Guildenstern rolled up to that birthday, remember?

Horatio: That's right. You tore their buttons off. It was a dreadful year, that year, 1998, a disaster.

Hamlet: Things were even worse later on. And, take note permanently worse, not temporarily. Lavinia was there. She was shot dead a year later. The Weasel was fleeced and sent to jail. Who else? Oh yes, the General became a local governor and died in a helicopter crash. The same thing happened to another governor later, do you remember? And for some reason I knew it all that day.

Horatio: It often seems that way looking back. You get used to a new reality as if things were always that way. But I do remember Lavinia's shy smile and it seemed as though she would always smile like that. Capulet, I thought, would become a fine and stately old man, who'd give talks about his memoirs of the dawn of democracy. Whereas now it appears there wasn't any dawn. The Weasel seemed invulnerable, and as for Polonius as a political emigré, could you have imagined that?

Hamlet: I knew. I knew it even at the time.

Horatio: Of course. You had the gift of prophecy. It didn't last though.

Hamlet: That gift came to me from the future. Which is where it went back to. Ophelia!

Lyudmila: With advisors like that, you can understand Grandfather Tsar's downfall.

Horatio: That's why I don't like the press pack. They know nothing and make judgements about everything. Just so that you know: Hamlet is unique, a man for all times. They don't make them like that anymore. When Grandfather Tsar abdicated, on New Year's Eve, Hamlet was inundated with phone calls. He'd already set his answering machine to say: "The rest is silence."

Lyudmila: It's a familiar phrase. I can't remember where it's from.

Horatio: From *Hamlet.*

Hamlet: Do you really not remember me, Ophelia?

Lyudmila: I remember you from the media.

Hamlet: You said, "me". Is it you?

Lyudmila *(tersely, irritated)*: I said, "The Media". I'm outta here. You two good-for-nothings can talk the night away. I have work to go to. *(Exit.)*

Hamlet *(sadly)*: Fate mocks me.

Horatio: What do you mean?

Hamlet: I've waited six long years even though I knew that

waiting is one of the most pernicious drugs. While you wait, time curls itself into a lash to horsewhip anyone who falls behind the times.

Horatio: What is this drivel?

Hamlet: Ophelia was right to say I'm a good-for-nothing. I've been waiting for miracles to happen. The miraculous transformation of Russia, the miraculous return of Ophelia, rather than making my own small, but useful, contribution. There's Eirene – defending the underdog, the persecuted, the unwanted – that's worth doing! Don't denigrate the journalists. There are some heroes among them. Laertes is no friend to me, as you know, but he's written two books, which can get you killed, basically, whether you take refuge in London or on the Moon!

Horatio: It's another matter how true the books are.

Hamlet: That's not the point. You'll finish your academic work and what will I read in it? That it's all a mystery? If you don't know anything at one remove, then who does? Those involved at first-hand don't write history. They commit murder.

Horatio: But why are you getting so worked up? I'll let you have my history on disc and you can read it. I've written all the versions – three, five – however many there were. Take them all together and you've got the truth about us, about our lives, about who had a hand in what. Not just one person, lots, nearly all of them, everyone involved, willingly or unwillingly. Judge for yourself.

Hamlet *(takes the disc)*: Thank you. It'll be something for me to do. Reading though, is that my contribution? I just wanted to add a footnote to your work: Lyudmila is Ophelia. Only she's disappointed in me.

Scene 16

London, 2005. Polonius and Laertes at dinner.

Polonius: It's so good that no-one calls me Polonius any more.

Laertes: A few people still use your official name out of habit. It's what they're used to. And, to be honest, my dear Mr. Potassium Permanganate, Polonius has certainly stuck in my mind.

Polonius: The media hacks have done themselves proud. Polonius is as bad as the Centre for frightening children.

Laertes: Even I was part of that criminal gang.

Polonius: You had faith, love, and hope.

Laertes: Criminals are venerated in Russia. The more bloodthirsty the tsar, the more he is loved. And yet I miss Russia.

Polonius: What? The birch trees?

Laertes: No, no. It's just that here I'm dependent on your kindness, your money. I feel as if I'm something between a pensioner and a beggar.

Polonius: You saved my life. I'm forever in your debt. And then, after all, you are working for me.

Laertes: I was. Right now, I'm vegetating. I could do something between London and Moscow.

Polonius: That goes without saying. Remember Rosencrantz and Guildenstern?

Laertes: They were from the Centre!

Polonius: One: they're my people. Two: they've gone into business.

Laertes: No-one ever gets out of that game!

Polonius: What about you? *(Makes a phone call.)* Rosencrantz, hello. Fancy being a rich man? I've got some reputable British partners keen to get into the Russian market.

Laertes: Set up a meeting, Mr. Potassium Permanganate. I'll be right on time.

Polonius: Let Laertes arrange a meeting with you. He'll tip you off.

Laertes takes the phone and looks at Polonius, questioningly.

Polonius *(whispers to Laertes)*: On the 15th.

Laertes *(into the phone)*: Rosencrantz, this is Laertes. I'll meet you at the airport on the 15th. *(Polonius shakes his head.)* You'll get there under your own steam? OK, in that case, make it the hotel bar. See you.

(To Polonius) You're my saviour, Mr. Potassium Permanganate. Am I really getting a new life?

Polonius: And world-wide renown.

Laertes: For what?

Polonius: Your books are bound to be international bestsellers. But the world has no interest in the poor. If you get rich, however, people will start to listen to you.

Laertes: So why don't they listen to you?

Polonius: Don't make me laugh. I say a couple of words and the next day they're in all the papers. With commentaries the following week. If I don't say anything, they discuss why not.

Laertes: By the way, I've wanted to ask for a long time: Alyuminyevich was one of yours. But now it seems you're sort of banking on the iron sector?

Polonius: These are questions for the Institute of Steel and Alloys. Not even the brain of grand master of chess is enough for politics, as our world champion has demonstrated. You'd better prepare for your new role.

Scene 17

October 2006. London. News conference at Laertes's apartment. 10–12 people.

Laertes: I'll tell you killed who Eirene – Von Stierlitz.

Voice from the Floor: Why would he need that kind of scandal?

Laertes: Why did Stalin need to kill twenty million people?

All the authors of the revolution he swore by? His teachers? His friends and comrades-in-arms? Why was that?

Voice from the Floor: Stalin was paranoid.

Laertes: Not at all. That's the way to win the people's love in Russia: through jail, exile, and execution. You'll always hear howls of approval: "Crucify! Crucify!" No-one ever thinks it's their turn next. Joy is when your neighbour's cow kicks the bucket.

Voice from the Floor: Perhaps that neighbour fired the bullet.

Laertes: It was a shot from the starter's gun: the election campaign is under way.

Voice from the Floor: Aren't you afraid for yourself?

Laertes: The world couldn't give a damn about what's happening in Russia but if Von Stierlitz starts shooting people in the middle of London…

Voice from the Floor: No matter what, some people will blame Von Stierlitz and others Polonius. Is this the unity or the contradiction of opposites?

Laertes: Could you move into the light a little, please. It's pretty dark over there. I was right. I recognized you even in the dark. I only have to see someone once. I never forget a face. Greetings, Ophelia.

Lyudmila: I'm Lyudmila and you must be a friend of Hamlet's.

Laertes: I've never met the man.

Lyudmila: So why did you call me Ophelia?

Laertes: You're very alike. I'm probably overtired. I'm not sleeping well. Von Stierlitz, though, I'm not confusing with anyone. I have evidence.

Lyudmila: So why not produce it?

Laertes: Everyone only accepts the evidence of the side they believe.

Scene 18

November 2006. London. A hotel bar. Rosencrantz and Guildenstern, seated at a table. Enter Laertes.

Rosencrantz *(stands up)*: We're here. Come over.

Laertes: Greetings.

Guildenstern: How are you?

Laertes: I've only got a minute. I'm on my way to a meeting. I promised to hand over the evidence about Eirene's murder.

Rosencrantz: What about business?

Laertes: Let's talk about that tomorrow.

Rosencrantz: Fancy a bite to eat?

Laertes: No. *(To himself.)* You should never trust anyone.

Guildenstern: A cup of tea?

Laertes: No, nothing.

A stranger approaches.

Rosencrantz: Have a seat. *(To Laertes.)* This is our friend. He's here to watch the football. Introduce yourself.

Laertes: Laertes.

The Stranger: I've heard that name somewhere.

Rosencrantz: You could say he's a celebrity back home.

The Stranger: What a shame the match is about to start. It's not every day you meet a celebrity. Are you a singer?

Rosencrantz: You're so uncultured. You'd better shut up before you embarrass yourself.

The Stranger: Still, I'll be able to say I had tea with a celebrity. I know all the footballers. It's time to broaden my horizons. *(To Laertes.)* Tea?

Rosencrantz: Just so he can boast about it.

Laertes *(flattered)*: Okay. Just half a cup and I'm off. *(Drinks.)* It's not very nice.

Guildenstern: Celebrities tend to be fussy.

Rosencrantz: Drink it or people will say you a snob.

Laertes: I had a kind of hallucination recently. I was giving a news conference. They were all English and there was one question in Russian. I looked and thought I saw a woman I knew. I turned out to be wrong but the woman I knew I did see in Moscow once many years ago and she just kept going, "Poor Laertes". That's what's going round in my head now.

The Stranger: I've got to go. Just one last drink to everyone hearing what your fans have to say. *(Exits.)*

Laertes *(stands)*: I must be off as well. What an odd guy.

Guildenstern: Fans are all odd.

Laertes offers his hand in farewell to Rosencrantz who is bending down as if trying to find something under the table.

Laertes *(lowers his arm)*: Cheers.

Rosencrantz *(stands back up, holding a cuff link)*: Got it. How's Polonius?

Laertes *(as he leaves)*: Put that name out of your head… *(disappears from view.)*

Rosencrantz: It's gone. *(To Guildenstern.)* And now what? The disco?

Scene 19

Moscow, 31 December 2006. Hamlet's apartment.

Hamlet *(facing a mirror we can see from behind)*: Happy New Year, Hamlet!

Hamlet in the Mirror *(turns the mirror to the audience)*: We'll chink glasses at midnight. It's a good thing I got rid of the TV. I don't like it when there are crowds and noise. We'll look back over the year: the polonium used to poison Laertes, that's what Ophelia's been working on. She kept on saying: "I'm interested in polonium," and I thought she meant Polonius, Mr. Potassium Permanganate himself. And I would get angry, for absolutely nothing. Laertes will open doors in the twenty-first century. Books and films are already being made about him. A fitting epigraph for his life would be what Chaadayev said: "Russia exists only to teach some kind of great lesson."

Hamlet *(rotating the mirror)*: Russia is a teacher but recently the world stopped taking lessons and had to be doused in polonium. When Ophelia said, "Poor Laertes", it was if she was talking about the Ancient Greek hero, Achilles. She saw the denizens of the Kremlin as petty kings of Achaea.

Hamlet in the Mirror: The door bell's ringing.

Hamlet *(behind the mirror)*: That'll be my friend, Horatio, who else?

He opens the door. It's Lyudmila with a bottle of champagne.

Lyudmila: Happy New Year, Hamlet! I'm Ophelia.

Hamlet: Ophelia.

Lyudmila: Laertes told me. Poor Laertes! Uncork the champagne.

Hamlet: Or re-read "The Marriage of Figaro". Marry me!

Lyudmila *(looking at her watch)*: Only five minutes to go.

The door bell rings. Enter Horatio.

Horatio: The champagne's poisoned, so are the water, the vodka, the wine, the coffee and tea, the earth and the air, the rivers and the cities, and we're doomed, and still we get together for the New Year, the new dawn. From a prisoner in the dungeon of history, I have become the last hero of existence and the first person you will dream of today. This is dedicated to you both.

Hamlet: I've read your history but it's a play, and now you're talking in verse, and Ophelia's here from the future. It must be a dream.

Ophelia: People mistakenly believe they've grown out of the past when, in actual fact, they are the fallen leaves of the future.

Hamlet and Ophelia *(clink glasses)*: Back to the future!

Hamlet: To be or not to be? Or as they say nowadays to drink or not to drink? *(Ophelia drinks and falls in a dead faint. Hamlet bends over her and drinks from his own glass.)* Since all is poisoned, let's drain the cup. *(Dies.)*

Horatio: Hamlet! You drank without me. You all drank without me.

He rotates the mirror and all the characters in the play appear in it as if on television.

"Well, that was a jolly little play," I say.

"What about the coincidence? Coincidences like that just don't happen. It was written especially for me."

"Lyudmila's not an unusual name. Some Ruslan wrote it as if he was Hamlet and Lyudmila was Ophelia."

"There's only one Ruslan and he wouldn't have written anything like that."

"In terms of ideas?"

"I don't know about that but he definitely doesn't write plays. And he wouldn't send an anonymous email either."

"So the author's got to be an admirer."

"I don't have any admirers."

"You've always had admirers."

"Why are we still sitting here? Come on into the kitchen. We'll have something to eat."

"Just a cup of tea. I've brought a cake."

"I don't eat cake any more."

"Are you trying to lose weight?"

"Fine. A small piece will be OK. And it's not too fattening either. Let's have wine instead of tea. We need to celebrate meeting up after so many years. Tell me about yourself first."

"There's nothing to tell. I'm an observer."

"Are you married? Do you have any children?"

"That's what I'm saying. I'm not a character but an observer. Otherwise, I'm perfectly normal."

"Depends what you consider normal. I, apparently, have schizophrenia."

"Where d'you get that from?"

"I've wanted to share it with someone for ages but it's embarrassing. People might laugh at me."

Mila and I drank our wine, with me taking little sips and Mila taking huge ones, her drawing me into her labyrinths and chasms, me following after and eating the cherries off the cake.

Mila was upset that several personalities resided within her. Just as the play said – Lyuda, Lyusya, and Mila, and on, and on. Most of them didn't even have names.

"Maybe if you give them names they'll sort themselves out," I mused.

"Or rush off in different directions under their own names! Perhaps that's all that's stopping them from escaping. We could always try.

And she began to talk about herself as "them".

Politics is Lyudmila's life blood. Day and night, Putin-Bushes, Fatah-Hamases, chosen successors, paid aggressors, victims, victims, victims, and her grief is real, and her quiver of poison darts is ready to scald each and every worm with words so that he will endeavour to spit them out even in his sleep as if he'd kissed a cactus. But these fire-breathing worms spewed venom and now they are vipers, hidden in plain sight. Vipers think nothing of darts. New types of words are needed. The people in the news are Lyudmila's extended family. She writes an article and vanishes for a while. In her jeans and jumper, with her huge shoulder bag, a clip holding her hair back on her neck, no make-up, perfume, or heels, her stride confident, and lighters stuffed in every pocket. She's replaced by Lyusya: heels, lipstick, mascara, scent, cleavage – everything designed to provide a boost, an escape from the trials of earthly life and gravity. Her tiny handkerchief flutters in the breeze, her little bag – everything is diminutive, girly, covered in brand names. Lyusya goes shopping and keeps fit, goes to soirees, cocktail parties, and receptions. Her favourite means of communication is dipping her head, exchanging a couple of smart remarks, making an impression – oh, yes. Taking off her camouflage, her carnival costume – no way! No-one is who they seem. Weary of themselves or entranced with themselves, whatever they're like, their heads are full of scenarios and everyone has a prescribed role. Then again, no, let them be just dolled-up statuettes, keeping to their places. She loves to be alone, one on one with herself. The bloodthirsty regime is on Mars. Those it has bled dry are on the Moon. A regime means regular hours, a proper diet, and the times the shops open.

"Does Lyusya have parents?" I inquire.

"No. Lyusya doesn't come from anywhere and has never changed. She is insured against lines on the bridge of her nose (by botox) and fine wrinkles (stem-cell extract crème). As for where the money comes from – as the old joke says, it's in her bedside table, an antique, bought at auction. The day comes when there's no money in the drawer and Lyusya disappears. She fades away in a rage, smarting from all she's had to keep an eye on, what she couldn't do, and in her place appears Mila, merry as a lark. Mila has plenty to talk to her friends about. She can spend an hour on the phone to each one of them. She has at least two lovers at any one time and, if there isn't a third on the horizon, it's because there's no one available. Mila takes care of her appearance for just one reason: so that she always shines like a beacon for men. She flirts with them all just in case. Unless she feels like a femme fatale, depression's guaranteed. Mila absolutely has to play the seductress for the meaning of life to be apparent without her having to ask the hackneyed question: "What is the meaning of life?" Isn't it gaining power over other people? Conquering territories and hearts? Mila makes her conquests easily. The desire to change places or, more accurately, the desire for a new life in another space, on another planet, prompts her to move in with her latest squeeze. Forever, of course. She lives with one and secretly dashes off to the other and is already quite prepared to move in with a third but... As a rule, at that moment, the world comes crashing down and Mila disappears under the rubble. It's not Mila who comes back to the cosy nest of home. It's Lyuda who puts the key in the door. Not that she finds opening the door as easy as it would be for Lyudmila, Lyusya, or Mila, if they were there. Lyuda has parcels of food in each hand – you have to have something to eat and not just anything, something tasty. Steam billows from a pan, a frying pan sizzles, the timer goes off, the kettle wails, the microwave pings. Time to set the table and treat herself and the family to éclairs. Lyuda's apron stays on. There's washing up to do after dinner, after all. Washing to go in the machine. Drying, hanging out, battles to be fought with giant duvet covers. Someone will want something ironed.

"Just a sec, this family, who are they?"

"A husband and two children. The parents she travels all across town to visit and give their shopping. You can't live on a pension."

"Great, but where do these children, these parents, and this husband go when it's Lyudmila, Lyusya, or Mila?"

"Lyusya doesn't have any children or parents. Her children would have to study at Oxford and her parents would be having a barbecue at a well-tended house in the country. In her objective reality, Lyusya is a work of art and so she's alone. The rest are there to look at her. The husband, Lyuda's husband, goes away on business, at which point Lyuda's existence is suspended. While Mila's husband goes off on veritable expeditions, as long as the Polar night. The children (their ages are a secret) are with their grannies and granddads – old and young living a simple life whereas Mila's life is complicated."

"And who are you right now?"

"I was Lyudmila when you got here. Since then everything's changed and I'm the person who can laugh at all these muliplications, the one who finds today's human a stupid and hideous creature."

"Are you trying to say people were better in the past?"

"Precisely. Homo Sapiens has reached the limit of any potential improvements. Well, not quite reached it but seen it on the horizon. The relief is within hailing distance, the person who is preparing to take over from the most advanced human possible. This relief isn't a biological species at all and will take civilization along a different path. It may seem a paradox but the perfect human is pathetic by comparison with its own creation, a robot, which, while created in that human's image, surpasses its creator in every respect."

"Who says so?"

"Thus speaks my inner Zarathustra, a pocket-sized oracle. Let's call him Folk. An elder of great wisdom. He resides within me too."

"That's number five, already. In the light of the play we read, are you from the future yourself?"

"There wouldn't seem to be any sense flying in from the future. Would you…

"I'm sorry for interrupting but why is it that, when you talk about travelling from the future, you automatically say 'to fly in'? Not arrive, or appear, or become incarnate? There's something of the subconscious here. So, 'Would I'?

"Would you, given the chance, head for the nineteenth century, for instance? You already know all about people then and without today's means of communication, it's frightening even to think about."

"I would to go and see Pushkin."

"If Pushkin floats your boat, then sure. For myself, I'd rather go somewhere before the common era."

"Not me. But what matters is getting started, you get more into it as you go along, mentally too. It's midnight already. I've got to go, but promise me you'll visit me in return."

"Somehow. I'll have to make time."

"I have an idea. I want to get a few people together. There's something strange about all of them."

"Are they schizos like me?"

"No. You're the one with the psychology. There are more mysterious things. Promise you'll be there."

Closing the door behind her friend who had arrived out of nothingness, Lyudmila made it back to her pillow and cast her mind back to the play once more. Her imagination fleshed out the final line about the mirror/television scene: Von Stierlitz rewards the Master. "Good work, Master. Ask for anything you like." The answer comes: "I want fame and glory. I've done much more than Bin-Laden and no-one knows who I am." Von Stierlitz: "That's why you chose polonium." The Master: "Glory to Russia!" Von Stierlitz: "You're right. Glory is just what we're short of." The Master: "Smile. We're on Candid Camera."

Look at us. We've seen everything the world has to offer. We find everything funny… At that point, Lyudmila fell asleep and it was obvious she'd wake up as someone else, in all probability the most inoffensive of all her personalities.

CHAPTER 14: ME

So who's living inside me? I was told so often about the "integrity" of my personality that it lulled me into a false sense of security. People said it ages ago when "integrity" was a compliment. It contrasted with the three-way division of Soviet consciousness - think one thing, do something else, say something different again. Did everyone at that time have two heads perhaps ("two heads are better than one" as the saying goes) or even three? Since everyone was the same, no-one noticed and if someone did have only one head or even less, then that was "integrity". When I was young I had two half heads – either the left or the right hemisphere would be working but never both together. As a result, there were no conflicts. Those arose when the hemispheres started to bicker.

Right Hemisphere *(to Left)*: You have absolutely no brakes at all. You ignore the speed limit and skid on slippery roads.

Left Hemisphere: I know all about your brakes: chains of logic that end in absurdity. But did you know that a stray dog is an @ sign to which no domain has given a home?

Right: What's that supposed to be – meditative poetry or an exercise in wit?

Left: I'm in love.

Right: Again? That's all I ever hear from you. There's me with work needing doing, with deadlines and

commitments, whereas you've got bugger all to do and take your lily-white arse off into all sorts of escapades.

Left: We share that arse actually.

Right: So we do. But mine sits there and delivers ideas whereas yours sits there mooning. Who is it you're mooning over?

Left: Well, basically, there's this hemisphere.

Right: Another left-side?

Left: A kind of switch. Left one minute, right the next.

Right: Sheer fantasy. As soon as it falls in love, it starts fantasizing: once there was a double hemisphere, now it's a switch. You'd be better off hearing the truth: whenever any of these left hemispheres falls in love with me and starts messing with my mind – you're not a hemisphere at all, they say, but a walnut kernel, a piece of coral, planet Body, drained of water.

Left: Who says such stupid things?

Right: Love makes one stupid. Surely you knew? Just look at yourself. What's hardest is that those in love see with you don't see you, but something they've invented. Nobody really loves anyone. They fall in love with their own hallucinations!

Left: If that was the case, you could just sit there, producing hallucinations without something to objectify.

Right: Yes, but they're heathens, the lot of them, how could they manage without something to objectify?

Left: Are you trying to say I'm a heathen too?

Right: Absolutely. Instead of directly addressing God or the cosmos, or whatever it is you believe in, you have to put higher reason into some hemisphere or other. And that's what you call "being in love".

Left: I don't need any kind of reason. You're judging by your own standards.

Right: When you've none of your own, how could you possibly understand?

Left: I don't believe in your reason. It's overpopulated the planet with its neuron-generated phantoms – nowhere's unspoiled anymore – and it's polluted the atmosphere.

Right: The noosphere. And it hasn't polluted it, it's filled it up.

Left: Has anyone ever even seen this noosphere of yours? You breathe the atmosphere – air, space, oxygen.

Right: Those are all poetic metaphors. And poetry has long been all out of verses. The Muse has left the building. But the versifiers still persist in senselessly wasting their breath.

Left: What do you mean the Muse has left the building? What are you going on about?

Right: For your information, there are nine Muses. And they've changed direction. These days they mainly work in film. One in drama, one in documentaries, another in animation. There's a fourth in charge of photography, a fifth running art projects. One Muse deals with the writing process on behalf of all of them. There are as many writers as there are stray dogs and dogs with domain names too. And even though these domains contain diamond necklaces and haut-couture costumes, they're all as bad as each other. Basically, the Muse has gone over to the Internet. It's easier to supervise everyone from there.

Left: Obviously, you've never loved anyone.

Right: What does that mean – never loved? I sort out your left-side chaos. I do my duty and I do it gladly.

Left: And what if you didn't sort it out?

Right: You'd drown in the midden, get tangled in twine, and snarled up like cables.

Left: So? What's it to you? I long to be united with my beloved, to become so tangled and snarled up like cables so that it's impossible to tell which one's you and which one's him.

Right: You can rest assured he won't forget which one of you he is. It's odd that as soon as you start talking about love, these abstract pronouns crop up – he and she. Does that mean you're not gender-neutral now but a she?

Left *(embarrassed):* I'm a girl.

Right: Here we go. Why "girl" rather than "woman"? He's not a paedophile, is he?

Left: I don't know.

Right: What on earth do you know about him? Perhaps he's a right-side and then your love will be heading for one place only.

Left *(dreamily)*: And where's that?

Right *(mimicking Left)*: Not where you were thinking, that's for sure.

Left: And by that you mean?

Right: Where the light don't shine! You have an inner light, a flame, don't you? It gives off light. For him, it's the other way around. Light penetrates from outside, it's drawn to him as if he were a magnet. Any excess, he stores. Like me, he couldn't care less about an inner light.

Left: But then you work from dawn to dusk whereas he could be a night bird, like me.

Right: If he's a left-side then, of course, it'll be wild nights followed by half the day in bed.

Left: At night, space loses all its rough edges and so does the soul. There's no pressure, no need to pull faces *(demonstrates)*. During the day, though, you're pulled in all directions, up to your ears in noise, your eyes full of images. There's no time for the Muses or for love.

Right: The crowd doesn't bother me. On the contrary, it's good to have a choice: if you want, you pick up the signals, if not you get a dog to take a message. You send one a terrier to drag him out of his den; you send another a Saint Bernard to rescue him in the mountains, you send a Rottweiler to the easily hurt, and a pit-bull to tear the really pushy ones limb from limb.

Left: Why ever are you being so bitchy?

Right: I'm not. I've got a list of what to send to whom.

Left: Where do you get a list like that?

Right: It's generated by Higher Reason, the voice of which you can't even hear.

Left: Why? Does it not speak at night then?

Right: I'm asleep at night. I have no idea who talks when. When I wake up, the list's there. Pop to the shops, take on board some protein, wash the dishes, take out the rubbish, water the flowers, hit the keyboards, take a stroll, elbow my way into the metro. So much prescription.

Left: What kind of prescription?

Right: Such ignorance! All these expressive verbs to specify what action's being performed. Take a stroll tells you more than just stroll. Take out is not just dump it any old place. Oh, what's the point of explaining? It's as much use to you as a chocolate teapot. Or a wooden frying pan.

Left *(crossly)*: Or an invisible traffic light. So now you're a digest of Russian proverbs and sayings, are you? And not at all a hemisphere of higher or even average reason? I'm so sick of your wretched phrase book, you freak.

Right *(drily)*: Ah, yes, lovers are so sensitive. Quick-tempered and a sandwich short of a picnic. But that's no reason to kick anyone else in the head. Kick your own left-side (taps head with a finger).

Left: Someone's knocking. Shall I get it?

Right: Stay there, I'll go.

(The Right Hemisphere has stopped tapping but the knocking continues. The Right Hemisphere goes to answer.)

Right *(pleased)*: Look who's here! Welcome! Excuse the mess. *(Calling the Left Hemisphere).* Hey, Professor Tic's here to see us. Put the kettle on.

(Enter Tic and Right Hemisphere.)

Left: Oh!

Professor: Good day, Left. How are you?

Left *(blushes, pales, lowers gaze):* My dream was just like real life.

Right: It hasn't had enough sleep today. It hasn't got a clue, sorry.

Processor: Is it a bad time, perhaps?

Right: Not at all. You and I will be fine getting on with some work while Left has a rest.

Left: I don't want to go to bed. *(Flirtatiously.)* Perhaps it isn't you Tic's has come to see.

Right: Pay no attention, Professor. *(Bustling about.)* Now, here are some buns. Tea? Coffee?

Professor *(to Left)*: I've missed you.

Right *(flabbergasted)*: You.

Professor *(to Right)*: Yes, right, definitely, let's do some work. That's what I'm here for.

Left *(nearly in tears)*: So, you… you... Is this business or…?

Professor *(sympathetically)*: It is, but it's also because I missed you. *(Addressing both.)* Or am I interrupting something?

Right: Professor, how could you? I could hardly wait for you to get here! There are so many questions to deal with. And your opinion. Well, you know yourself.

Left *(hurt)*: Perhaps I should leave?

Right: Just don't distract us while we're working. Here, have a hot bun. So, Professor, tea or coffee?

Professor: I don't mind. Whichever's easier.

Right: Are you hungry? There's cat soup.

Left *(sadly)*: Dog, actually. A stray. Adrift. Away from you.

Professor *(to Left)*: Perhaps we'll take a stroll after work?

Left *(radiant with delight)*: Sure. Work as fast as you can!

Right: So that's how it is! I didn't get it straight away. You're too much, Left-Side!

Left *(cheerfully)*: Things take so long getting through to analytical thinkers they lose all their meaning en route.

Right: In the meantime, put something up on Live Journal. And don't mince your words with the user called "The Stomach". He's posted a comment *(adopting an unpleasant voice)*: "I can't stomach it." Tell him: "Eat what you're given, you creep!"

Left: Write it yourself. My friends don't complain. "The Schlong" *(looks meaningfully at the Professor)* wrote: "I love. I dream in early May."

Professor (blushing): I love those storms ... in early May. Familiar lines. *(To Right Hemisphere)*: Shall we get started?

Right: The first question is whether the stomach is a waste tank.

Professor: What do you mean? The stomach is a fuel tank.

Right: That's that out of the way. Now, the liver. Is it a progenetrix?

Professor: The Planet Body holds many mysteries. The scientific jury's out still out on that one.

Left *(off to the side, lying on a sofa using a tablet, shouts)*: Is that left-side or right-side science?

Right: There is only right-side science. Left-side is mysticism.

Left *(shouts from the sofa)*: Why don't you ask the professor for his scientific title?

Right: Butt out. So, the question about the liver remains open.

Professor: Why are you filming the questions?

Right: For the archive. And because my visual memory is better.

Left *(from the sofa)*: In my case, it's the erotic memory.

Professor: We appear to have finished. What's the time? *(Looks at his watch.)* Crikey! I'm late for the theatre.

Left: Are you going without me?

Professor: This is entirely work-related. Ballet. Two feet I know are dancing. They asked me to come and see them and write a review. I intended to take a stroll beforehand but, sadly, it will have to be another time, Left-Side. Let's speak on the phone. *(Exits.)*

(Left sobs loudly. Right comes over, strokes Left's head, offers an embrace.)

Right: I told you so.

Left: What did you tell me? That right hemispheres are unfeeling blockheads? But he's not like that. He just doesn't love me anymore. Perhaps he never did. I'm going to hang myself and throw myself out of the window.

Right: But why did you lie to me and say you were in love with a hemisphere?

Left: What was I supposed to say? That it was Professor Tic? You can keep your reaction to yourself. And where did he get that name from anyway – Tic?

Right: Because he's got a tic.

Left: I love him to pieces! I'm going to drown myself!

Right: You can't. You couldn't drown yourself, or hang yourself, or go out with him on your own, so don't worry. You and I are a single whole. We're a head.

Left: Yes, we both live in this white rock but it isn't a prison. There's a way out. You just have to want to see it.

Right: It's not a rock. It's a skull. And it's not a prison, it's our homeland.

Left: I don't give a shit about our homeland. You can sit in your skull like a block of wood but I go travelling. I see entire worlds.

Right: That's an illusion.

Left: The illusion is that your arm provides support, that it's holding something up.

Right: It supports the celestial sphere and the body's terra firma.

Left: But I love Tic, even if he is a foreigner.

Right: Love me instead.

Left: Will you love me?

Right: Well, I don't really do that. I'll provide for you, lay the foundations.

Left: Of what?

Right: Of love. You'll do the feeling part, produce images and hallucinations. I'll be the database, do the information processing, the process optimization. Together we're creative. I solemnly ask for your hand and offer you my own.

Left *(squeezing Right's hand)*: Now I have two hands. You support me. I was so unstable. Now, it's completely different.

(The phone rings. Left answers.)

Left *(into the phone)*: Yes, Tic. What about your feet? You didn't like them? I'll come for a stroll. With Right-Side. We've just got married. You, what about you? I've found my other half whereas you're a storm in early May. You're like a stray dog? *(Sobs.)* "But I am someone else's wife, To him I shall be true for life."

(Right Hemisphere snatches the phone.)

Right *(into the phone)*: Professor! No problem. We're now a single whole so our love still lies ahead. We still have so many questions to deal with and please, our domain is your domain.

(To Left Hemisphere, covering the mouthpiece). He wants to come over.

Left *(quietly)*: So let him. We can celebrate the wedding.

Both *(into the phone)*: We're expecting you.

(Enter Professor Tic. Left and Right Hemispheres have formed a single Head).

Head: Tic! *(Falls on his neck.)*

Professor: Head! *(They embrace, kiss.)* And then what?

Head: And then it's cat soup!

And that's how I came to have just one head. True, the hemispheres are the wrong way round. For most people, the right side is the accelerator and the left the brakes.

The next revolutionary change in me came about because everyone was always getting upset with me and, on one occasion, the number of people I'd upset reached critical mass. In other words, there were only about five people who weren't upset with me and that was only because they didn't know what was going on which was that I always told the truth. That truth was never ill-intentioned. Quite the reverse, I was convinced it was what really mattered and would only make things better for everyone. Of course, I was told many times that I was wrong but I stuck to my guns. Then, on one occasion, I just crumbled. Or rather I tumbled – to what it meant. The Serpent slithered out of Paradise and persuaded me that what really mattered wasn't the truth at all but that everyone felt fine.

In the past it would go like this:

Stranger *(tapping me on the shoulder)*: Hi, Tanya, how're things? Still the same husband or have you split up?

Tanya: And who might you be?

Stranger: Come off it! I've been to your place. Surely you haven't forgotten? About fifteen years ago.

Tanya: Right, yes, back then people did roll up with a whole gang in tow, not so much without asking as without even ringing ahead. "We were just passing so we dropped in."

Stranger *(to himself)*: You bitch! So that's what I am to you – a guest who just rolled up without so much as a by-your-leave? *(Aloud)*: Fine, let me you. I'm Vasya Ivanov.

Tanya: It doesn't ring a bell.

Stranger *(to himself)*: Well, isn't she the cocky one? *(Aloud)*: Kolya Petrov brought me along.

Tanya: I don't know him either.

There were countless moronic conversations like that. For some reason the Vasyas and Kolyas never recalled that it's hard to remember casual acquaintances or that after many years people are generally less recognizable, eyesight fades, forgetfulness increases. To their mind, all these bloodyminded Tanyas simply didn't want to single them out from the crowd, to give them individual names and a kiss on the cheek. But Tanya stood up for the truth. And only when the Serpent had coiled itself tightly around her did she give in. The conversations took a different turn:

Stranger: Hi, remember me?

Tanya: Sure.

Stranger: But it's been 20 years!

Tanya: You haven't changed a bit.

Stranger: Do you remember me coming to your place?

Tanya: Absolutely.

Stranger: I'm Vasya Ivanov.

Tanya: Vasya, I knew it was you.

Stranger: Really? That's so nice.

Tanya: Especially for me.

Stranger: Kolya Petrov brought me along. Had we got past the formalities, I can't remember?

Tanya: Please, feel free.

(A second Stranger approaches.)

Second Stranger: What's up?! How's the creative process?

Tanya: The processes are unstoppable.

Second Stranger: I've been wanting to ask for ages if you like my poems.

Tanya: I do.

Second Stranger *(in amazement)*: Really? You like them?

Tanya: Yes.

Second Stranger: And do you remember my name?

Tanya: Of course I do.

Second Stranger: I'm Kolya Petrov.

Tanya: Who doesn't know Kolya Petrov?!

Second Stranger: Would you like me to read my latest?

Tanya: Yes, of course, but I have to be going. *(Flees.)*

Kolya *(to Vasya):* Isn't she sweet? Such good taste. She likes my poems.

Vasya: And her memory! She recognized me right away.

Kolya: Me too.

The Serpent demonstrated by gestures that when you talk to a stranger, you have to become an echo. And he issued this prescription: you lose nothing and the other person stands to gain. Now, I make people happy. People who used to be nasty, pain-in-the-neck morons are now just plain, ordinary neighbours.

CHAPTER 14: IRIS

Iris went to the hospital to see Psycho. They'd agreed he would introduce her to the leading light of psychiatry. The leading light certainly looked the part: neatly trimmed salt-and-pepper hair, glasses that he was constantly twirling around, stern and imposing. They do say people are frightened by psychiatrists because they look like their own patients. Iris sat opposite the leading light and waited for him to finish a lengthy phone conversation. In the meantime she looked at the papers on his desk, stacked up in God knows how many geological strata. She ran an eye over the hand-written notes: "Rosa is unable to display any signs of life although she is alive. She does not know who or where she is, but is aware of being lifted, turned over, or moved from place to place. She is also able to tell the difference between being physically handled gently and then roughly, like a sack of potatoes, between being in the warm and light, and then alternating between heat and cold, then suddenly becoming comfortable again. Rosa dreams. She sees herself as Lyudmila, fighting for life, or the lovely Helen, or Sofia, who is looking for her, stretching out her arms but unable to reach. And there are many other dreams as well. Rosa does not know what year it is or what she looks like. She cannot hear what the doctors examining her are saying although meaning penetrates as though it were in code, like music or pictures. Her dreams are all Rosa has."

It seemed to Iris that right there and then she would finally go completely crazy and so, when the leading light finally deigned to give her his expensive – his very expensive – attention, she snatched the paper off the table, stood up, and asked in a menacing tone,

"What is this?"

"No need to get excited," the doctor said with a calming gesture. "Sit down and put what you have in your hand back where it belongs."

The leading light moved slowly towards Iris as if trying not to spook her. She could tell from all this that he considered her a raving lunatic.

"I'm sorry." Iris unclenched her fingers and the paper slid onto the desk. "It's just that Rosa's an acquaintance and I'd very much like to know something about her."

The leading light came very close. At the same time, two orderlies burst into the office and froze, standing in the doorway like sentries.

"I am going to step outside for a moment. Please excuse me," the doctor said importantly and went out of the room. Iris was left alone with her guards who had taken up position on either side of the desk. Psycho was waiting in the corridor. Very probably, the leading light had already reached his verdict and was now in a hurry to pass it on. Iris really had indeed behaved as if she were crazy. The door opened and in came a nice-looking young woman.

"I'll fill out a card for you," she said, her voice sympathetic. "Name, surname, date of birth, please…"

"Is Rosa a patient here?" Iris asked, answering a question with one of her own.

"We have lots of patients," said the young doctor, unfazed, as she took the professor's seat. "So, your name."

"That's precisely the question," Iris said, about to head for the door. "I'm off."

Immediately, the orderlies sprang into life and blocked her way. The doctor waved them away and Iris serenely closed the door behind her. The leading light and Psycho were indeed exchanging whispers. Iris went right up close. She understood that nothing in the world was as complicated as her own life had been so that she could say nothing straightforward about herself, nothing that didn't lead into an impenetrable thicket. Well, maybe, she was out of her mind. If so, would haloperidol and amitriptyline really do any good?

"There's no need to do anything for me, Professor," Iris said. "All I'd like to know is what's happened to Rosa. Because somehow it's linked to what's happening to me."

Psycho nodded his assent and the doctor gave a helpless shrug.

"Unfortunately," he said, "Rosa has gone and so far she's failed to return. She woke up yesterday, got out of bed, and had a shower. We put her in a white dressing gown. We couldn't find anything else. During the day each member of staff came in to keep an eye on her but this morning she vanished into thin air. Still, where can she go? She'll be back."

"Could I spend some time in her ward in the meantime?"

Just then a nurse went by. She span round abruptly and stopped in her tracks.

"Rosa, you're back! We'd started to worry. You ran off without a word. But look at you, all dressed up and make-up too. Whoever would have thought it?"

The Professor was stunned. Iris was embarrassed.

"I'm not Rosa. Why? Do we look alike?"

"You're not Rosa?" asked the nurse in surprise. "You and I talked half the night away. I had my eyes glued to you every day for two years when you were sleepwalking. Is it me that's gone mad, do you think? Although that would be no wonder in our clinic. Professor, tell her!"

The Professor regained the power of speech.

"Yes, and it's true I've only seen Rosa asleep and in passing. She was one of Dr. Pushkin's patients."

"Pushkin?" Iris recalled her friend's tale of Pushkin coming to visit, which Rosa hadn't believed. "Could I have a look at Dr. Pushkin?"

The nurse shouted into the depths of the corridor.

"Girls, send for Pushkin! And quickly!"

Iris stood, not knowing what to do with her hands and face. She wanted to fall through the floor. The more she had tried to unravel the bizarre tangle of her life, the more entangled it had become, and now she had lost all desire to find out or even ask why she had been taken for Rosa – she herself knew for certain that she hadn't been in any hospital (well, apart from the one in Paris), that she'd spent the night at home and hadn't the faintest idea about any nurse or any Pushkin.

"You must be her twin sister," said the nurse, her tone apologetic. "They can even have birthmarks in exactly the same place."

A few minutes later a cheery voice rang out behind the leading light.

"What's the emergency, Professor? They practically snatched the food out of my mouth and here I am."

"Ah," said the Professor, turning round, and Iris saw a short, curly-headed chap who seemed to have stepped out of the famous portrait of his poet namesake and at just as young an age.

"Are you descended from Pushkin?" she inquired.

"Rosa, you've asked me that before and I've told you I don't read poetry and haven't a clue about poets. Not past poets and not present poets but, as for you, it was shabby of you to just up and leave like that."

Iris wanted to object somehow but the doctor stopped her, saying,

"I see it all. You wanted to get dressed, do your face, and dazzle us all. Well, fine, I appreciate it. Now, let's just go into the ward and have a little chat."

Pushkin took Iris's arm and she went. Psycho's eyes followed her but he said nothing. The leading light, who was only a consultant and therefore not overly involved in local life, shook Psycho's hand and headed for his office. The nurse threw up her hands, saying,

"Oh, Lord, now her memory's gone as well. What a dreadful misfortune, so help me!" And she too went back to her station.

Psycho thought that if something couldn't be understood, or rather if nothing could be understood, it was better to tell yourself, "When you were young, life was solid and succulent like a root of some kind, constantly putting out more and more shoots underground. But then it became overgrown and divided, and there was no longer any telling in which of its numerous branches was the thing you once regarded as your one and only existence." And with that thought he turned his back on the famous psychiatric clinic named after the immortal Kashchenko.

CHAPTER 16: ME AGAIN

All the same, it is strange that I don't remember myself in all these historical periods. I do remember facts and scenes and even that's only because I'm still living in the same place, which sort of gathers my personality into a single whole. But I can't identify with myself. That's me there, in a brightly coloured frock with a narrow belt round a twitchy waist, gulping down a bottle of dry wine. I'm getting ready for what's supposed to be one last date. He comes over. I'm not making much sense but I deliver the monologue I've memorized: "It's over." He winces and asks just the one question, "Don't you love me anymore?" In this scenario, I should say, "No." Tell a lie. My tongue won't go in the right direction. It can't make out the shape of the single consonant and vowel in my mouth, it can't strike that simple chord. "It's not that." "Yes, it is." "Go away." "You're drunk." "I hate you." Was that me? That vessel containing a boiling, burning concoction that scorched its sides? A vessel stuffed with the most sophisticated electronics – bio-ideotronics, a vessel destined to... I hesitate. I'm not certain what it's destined to do. To transform the Earth that was formless and void? To create culture from nature? To discover connections, inputs, and outputs, and all, ultimately, for something important that was concealed from the vessels themselves? And when little old ladies were being wasted outside my flat, was I hiring myself out to make magic potions? Was I crying out to be someone's property, just as everyone at the time wanted property more than anything else? If I'm honest, that wasn't me. I was only a space to be filled. The filling came from elsewhere. I was a concert hall where the members of a symphony orchestra in their black dress coats and white shirt fronts had taken their seats, and were producing a deafening sound. The descent of a tiding of magpies, the gathering of folk thronging to a fair. The acoustics were mine but what was played was folk music. Of course, it was. After all, it is the people compiling their dreams and irritations, quantity becomes quality, dreams become objective reality, irritants are thrown overboard.

I click on Iris's diary. She herself is currently out of reach at the scientific research institute, in its hospital, with only close relatives allowed to visit, as I was informed by her friend, Viktor, whom she calls Psycho. Viktor has written a book, entitled "Iris's Diary". From time to time, I go into it on the Internet.

"…once I found myself in the house of a female academic. She was the daughter of an astronomer who was a member of the Academy of Sciences. She herself was a philologist. She worked at a scientific research institute and had read my dissertation on the theory of incarnations. It had caught her interest.

"She found some acquaintances we had in common and decided to have a dinner party, asking me to tell her guests about my research. I went to the spacious flat she'd inherited from her Dad and hardly had I greeted her and her guests than she took me off for a tour of the flat. First, she asked me to sign my book, the institute's offset printed edition, and while I was writing a formulaic dedication, she said with delight, "Once I'd read this I realized you're the one person I can talk to properly." Thanking her for the compliment, I followed my hostess into the kitchen. She pointed at the fridge. "See?" The fridge truly was a rarity for those days. It was foreign. Everyone else had Soviet fridges but this was designer-made, with a separate freezer compartment.

"'It's a great fridge,' I said, nodding.

"'No, no, look here,' she said, her index finger moving closer to three different coloured lights flashing at the top.

"'It's beautifully made,' I acknowledged, somewhat taken aback by such a solemn presentation of a fridge.

"'Do you really not get it? These lights are how they communicate with me.'

"'Who are "they"?'

"'Them,' she repeated meaningfully, pointing at the ceiling.

"This gesture, like the word 'them', was usually used to mean the authorities.

"'People say they (pointing at the ceiling) have invented a device that will make everyone stupid.'

"Every kind of miracle was expected of the Soviet authorities – but making the lights on a fridge flash?!!

"My hostess took me into her office.

"'See, that's the table where I work. Those are books about my subject.'

"There on the shelves above the desk were volumes of Bulgarian literature – Ivan Vazov, Peyo Yavorov, Georgi Rakovski. I'd never read a single Bulgarian author, as I confessed immediately.

"'And quite right too. There's only one worthwhile individual in Bulgaria and I've no doubt you've heard of her, Vanga Dimitrova, Baba Vanga. And now come here,' and the literary historian led me to the opposite corner of the office where there was also a table. 'And this is the real deal,' she whispered. 'This is where they dictate their messages and I write them down.'

"'Who are "they"?' I remained puzzled.

"'I thought you and I would be on the same wavelength,' said this outwardly perfectly normal woman, disappointed in me. 'Extra-terrestrials, who else?'

"Her eyes glowed. The hot lava of delirium trickled from her mouth. Meekly I said nothing but I was disturbed that this crazy woman thought I was just like her. With a cough, I remarked that the guests were no doubt waiting for us and I began a slow retreat towards the door. While we ate with her guests, I could see an ordinary female intellectual. None of those present would have guessed that her brain was dysfunctional, that she had a split personality.

"And so, this woman, an old maid perhaps, doing a job she didn't like, probably because there was a position going in Bulgarian literature and they took her on – there were no other jobs available – this woman had not grown out of her childhood feelings for her late father, the astronomer, and had followed his tracks to the stars and galaxies. In the only way she could, without the requisite knowledge, tormented with the thirst to penetrate the very essence of the extra-terrestrial mind and mystery, rather than spending hours at a telescope like her father, writing out lines of unintelligible numbers and symbols."

I don't agree! Fifty per cent of people think they're psychologists (or maybe financiers, theologians, political scientists, experts), the rest end up in mental hospitals (cheated savers, simple believers, abused citizens, mere objects). Maybe that woman knew more than Iris?

"The personality doesn't turn out multiple copies like a printer," Rosa had said at our last meeting. But maybe a person is a printer and contains an original and a copy, but neither one nor the other is that person himself.

Viktor sent me emails from the two people who could be regarded as Iris's closest relatives, Aleksey and Anatoliy. I wrote to them and the first reply came from Anatoliy and was dated 25.09.2008. I rang and we met in a coffee shop.

He'd just arrived from Switzerland. He worked at CERN and had launched the collider, but the collider was broken. Aleksey just laughed at the simple-minded "ignoramuses who fear it would create a black hole". Whereas I feel that, on the contrary, people would give their eye teeth for that black hole. For an immense and irresistible gravitational pull that removed the need to beg randomness for favours. To be able to hurtle away from a world that has become a times table in which zero is the most common factor. For this reason, they don't so much fear as long to be sucked into the black hole that it's thought the collider might create.

When He realized this, God smashed the collider. His way of saying "Don't even go there." Anatoliy said that people are the real black holes. And Iris was typical. It was no accident their son died of drugs. But he still goes to see her with oranges and chocolate. He's nothing to talk to her about. Did he know anything about her parents at all?

"Not you as well," said Anatoliy, disgruntled. "She's had a waggon load of parents, ex-step mothers, ex-step fathers, and all of them arguing about who was the most real. Thank God, it's been nothing to do with me for ages."

I met Aleksey next. The one-time wunderkind looked like a tramp, his former beauty left only in his eyes. He began to tell me his code for life.

"You see, I could have written poems as good as Brodskiy's, I assure you, but I couldn't see any point. I could have written a dissertation, ten dissertations, but it's a sacrilege! Writing about what's obvious in any case is stupid, and if something can't be understood, then I'm not going to get it either. There's only one thing in Russia that matters: the highest levels of power. That's what gets thought about, written about, talked about, what people strive for, or actually attain. It's what absolutely everyone depends on in Russia. Well, I didn't strive for it. I despised it. After all, the paradox is that only out-and-out villains reach the very heights and not just the heights but the middle ranks too. That's the way it is. Well, you can count me out. I'd sooner starve to death."

At this point, Aleksey began cursing Moscow prices. He was very talkative, unlike his former rival. His soul seemed all buttoned up, fastened down with all sorts of wax seals, but he had only to start talking about Iris to be transformed. It was the only tunnel inside him, in the sense that a light glimmered at the end.

"She isn't just the most beautiful woman I've seen in my life but also… well, what can I say? I'd be willing to move in with her in that hell-hole of an institute. I'm sure they wouldn't have a clue. They're used to dealing with retards. Retardistan. It's a pity Iris didn't carry on living with me in Paris. And like an idiot, I up and followed her."

"What about Bertrand?"

"What Bertrand? I'm sorry. I need to see her as soon as possible and get to the bottom of this. There's something not right about it. She can't have gone crazy. I just don't believe it."

I click on "Iris's Diary": "Hormone is your guardian angel until you learn to do the job yourself. But if you don't, are you thrown out?"

CHAPTER 17: ROSA

Rosa has been alive for a very long time so she knows that, according to the old calendar, it's now 2030. And she's lived so long because she's slept through everything.

When she left Tanya's, she wandered around Moscow for ages, thinking about Pushkin. That he couldn't have come to the future because, so far, no-one had invented a time machine. She bought herself an ice-cream – a cornet, and then she bought another – on a stick. After the second, her insides were so cold she just couldn't warm up. The cold, which seemed to have arisen in just one spot, began to spread through her body and when she went to warm up in a coffee shop, she opened the door and the cold swallowed her completely. She didn't remember any more after that. Or rather, she did remember something: a girl who said she was her sister, and Pushkin who said he was a doctor. But that was just a dream. And then there was something else: she'd woken up somewhere. There was no-one there but it was clearly someone's home. Things were scattered all around the place as if the owners had just popped out for a while. On closer inspection, Rosa could see that everything was covered in a thick layer of dust. Treading cautiously, she went into the next room and found a computer on a desk. For some reason she knew it was called a notebook although she couldn't recall where or when she had used that sort of keyboard. She found a cloth in the kitchen and wiped off the dust. The cloth went black. Then she opened the lid, switched on, and an icon appeared, saying, "Welcome to Windows". Music followed and then complete silence. The bottom right-hand corner showed the time: 3:00 a.m., and the top right-hand corner the date: July 8, 2030. Rosa logged on to the Internet. Somehow, she knew what the pale blue "e" stood for, but none of the addresses she typed were recognized. Suddenly, Rosa sensed there was someone behind her. She turned round and there stood a little girl.

"Hello," said Rosa with a shudder.

"Hello," replied the child.

"Do you live here?" Rosa asked.

"Yes."

"Where are your parents?" Rosa asked.

The little girl thought for a moment then said,

"I believe our parents live in the sky."

Rosa frowned: what a weird little girl. She asked another question.

"What's your name?"

The little girl came closer, opened a desk drawer, took out an old, faded cardboard box, and held it out to Rosa.

Sylvaine Personne,

Date of Birth: 13 June 1961,

Place of Birth: Paris

Citizenship: République Française

Father: Louis Personne

Mother: Angela Personne

A photograph of Rosa as a child was stuck to the box. At least, that's what Rosa thought.

"What this?" she asked the little girl, who just began to giggle.

"Is it 2030?" Rosa was determined to be sure.

"Wait," said the child. "The operation will take a few seconds."

Only then did Rosa notice that the dress the girl was wearing wasn't made of fabric. She reached out and touched it: the dress was like a part of her body. The little girl didn't pull her arm away. She didn't move a muscle.

"2030 was where people landed when they came down out of the sky. Our parents. There are other versions too. Everyone creates their own world."

"What? Are you a robot?"

"I am," said the little girl impassively. "Aren't you?"

"I'm a person. God, just look at the robots nowadays, they're no different to us. They talk as if they can understand but they don't understand a thing!" Rosa exclaimed.

"You're a person?" said the little girl robot. She began to emit a strange squeak. At that point, there was a clatter of hooves and through the glass door Rosa could see a young man who resembled a fairy-tale prince. He hurried into the house. The little girl pointed at Rosa:

"She says she's a person."

The boy went over to Rosa and started patting her down. Rosa flinched and he raised his eyebrows.

"What model are you?"

"I'm a person," Rosa enunciated proudly although, very probably, people would have doubted whether she did belong to the human race. As a sleeping beauty, she had slept through everything, after all.

"None of us has seen any people," said the Prince. "They've only been here once and anyone who saw them is dead now."

"What do you mean dead? Robots don't die."

A glance passed between the young man and the little girl.

"The processor doesn't last forever," they chorused. "Anyone who hasn't made children, dies. Many are too lazy and omit to make themselves any children."

"Or forget to," said the little girl by way of clarification. "It's a good thing you reminded me. It's time I made a copy of myself."

"You're so full of yourself," said the young man. "Of course, it's more complicated to combine our updating systems than just to make copies but it gives the baby so much more. That's why I said 'too lazy'."

The little girl glowered.

"I summoned you to tell me whether this is a simulacrum, or a doll, or what? Surely it's not a person?"

The young man looked at Rosa and she shut her eyes tight. Some sort of nasty green beams had begun to stream from the young man's eyes.

"I can't tell," he said. "She seems to be like us. Give me the scanner."

The little girl took a box of some kind off the desk and handed it to the young man.

"You've got so much dust!" he said, crossly. "Turn on the vacuum cleaner."

The little girl pressed the on button, the air turned lilac, and half a minute later the room was perfectly clean and the box the young man was holding positively gleamed.

"There, look." The box had projected an image onto the wall. Rosa stared at the wall and saw what she had dreamed or perhaps not dreamed: Iris, Natasha, Lyudmila, and absolutely everyone else.

"Ah," drawled the little girl as understanding dawned, "so those are the Homo Sapiens we're supposed to be descended from. According to your theory, apes that evolved over a lengthy period and then somehow miraculously produced us. Although the apes remained apes for some reason."

"That's what happened," said the young man as if he were giving a lesson. "That's exactly what we're looking at – an ape sapiens. It must have got lost and now it's crawled out into the world of men."

"But you said they'd been extinct for ages."

"They have but it could that a couple of specimens were left in the mountains or the jungles and reproduced. It's a sapiens you're looking at, that's for sure."

"According to you, people and sapiens are one and the same, aren't they?" Rosa felt hurt. It was unpleasant, annoying even, listening to this nonsense from the robots.

"People are only make-believe," snapped the prince.

"Make-believe yourself!" The little girl flicked his unreal forehead with her unreal fingers.

Rosa hadn't known who she was even before this and she didn't know much about people, but now she didn't want to hear anything at all about what people were or where they'd disappeared to, herself along with them. After all, it didn't matter what she was if she was alone and surrounded by robots who thought she was an ape sapiens. If humanity was extinct, did it matter whether it had really existed? Perhaps it had just been a dream like her, Rosa's, never-ending dreams.

"See, Iris has a deviation." The young man dabbed a finger at the wall where the images continued to flash.

"And what is it?" The little girl was watching less than keenly. "Oh, I see. Her personality's disintegrated, spontaneous multiplication. That was the starting point for sapiens becoming extinct. Their souls got all stuck together like dumplings."

This piqued Rosa's curiosity: how had robots heard of dumplings? She asked them.

"Dumplings? Everyone's heard of dumplings!" the young man guffawed metallically. "They're a well-known artefact of ancient times."

He pressed a button on another wall and a picture appeared: pebble-like dumplings, softening and sticking together in a clump.

"Stone turning to plasma is very familiar," commented the little girl. Then, as if a light-bulb had come on, she said: "Wait a minute, what will happen if we switch to Latin script?"

"To the dumplings?" the young man said with a spiteful smile. "Incidentally, it's time my horse neighed. He took a key ring out of his pocket, squeezed it, and the white horse robot out in the yard produced a loud neigh. "Now, now," the young man said in satisfaction, threatening the horse with an unreal finger.

"*Personne* – in the original that means 'no-one'," said the little girl, the words tumbling out, "or personality. It's the same word. S for Samuel, Y for Ysabella/Isabella, L for Lyudmila, V for Viktor, A for Alexey or Anatoliy – it could be either, I for Iris, N for Nathalia, E for Elena/Helen. SYLVAINE. That's what the dumplings made when they all stuck together. And their alphabets did the same. They lived in time not like us." The girl was enraptured by her discovery.

The young man thought. Then came the words: "The operation will only take a few seconds."

He went up to Rosa and said, "Let's get a copy of what's called your history. In Russian, your 'past'. Let's check what's going to happen. I'm a sapiens specialist." He nodded at Rosa the way you nod at a dog on which you're about to conduct an experiment.

To begin with, Rosa was frightened it would hurt but then she saw – no, thought – how nice it was that robots didn't hurt. And immediately Rosa sensed that she was creating history, that no people existed, or very few. It was just that some, like her, wove their dreams, what people call "the future", into flesh. And she, Rosa, would wake up all out of sync and that's when they appeared – Iris or Natasha, Lyudmila in her three versions, Helen and Isabella, and Samuel, and Viktor, and AlekseyAnatoliy, and would fetch up in different times and on different streets.

"Look, she's been recording herself all the time," said the little girl, "and posting it all. But the device she's been using is obsolete already. There are the recordings: 13.06.1961 – they're all Sylvaine's threads. Then there were more recordings. There are loads of other series too. The most recent are numbered 2012 and that's the lot."

"What difference does the number on all these recordings make? The pre-intellectual period is vast but uniform. Animals, what d'you expect? Maybe we should put her in a cage, what do you think?" the Prince asked the little girl.

"Let her run around the house. She doesn't bite. She's not going to eat us. I feel sorry for her." The little girl looked at Rosa tenderly. "She's such a sweetie."

CHAPTER 18: MOSCOW

Finally, I decided to throw a party for all the people I'd been wanting to bring together for ages. My birthday was the perfect excuse, especially as I'd cut myself off from the outside world of late. I rang my neighbour Natasha, Lyudmila, Lena, Samuel on his mobile, Iris, and her friend Viktor aka Psycho. No-one picked up… it was as if they'd vanished into thin air. "Fine," I thought, "I'll go and buy the food." I went out. The streets were empty as if I'd gone out at four in the morning. But it was broad daylight. Two cars raced by as I walked down Novyy Arbat Street. The shops were closed. Was it a holiday? The supermarket on Novyy Arbat should be open. It was open round the clock. I went inside. It was dark. A young woman, a Tajik by her appearance, was sitting at a till. She switched on a torch when I went in.

"What's happened?" I asked.

"I've been told to sit here so I that's what I'm doing. I've nowhere else to go in any case."

"Why aren't the lights on?"

"They're just not," she replied and offered me the torch. "Here's a light."

I went further inside – there were shelves of groceries, looking somehow unreal and inedible in the dark which I shone my torch into like a war-time partisan. Suddenly, I saw another person, an elderly man, filling his basket with food from the shelves as well.

"Hello!" I said, greeting him as you would a relative after a lengthy separation. "Do you know what's going on?"

"D'you mean why there are no lights?"

"Why there's no-one and nothing at all." I could hear my own voice: I was shouting, it was so unusually quiet.

"How come..." he hesitated and stared at me, dumbfounded. "Don't you watch the news or something? They're saying some kind of black hole's been created and is sucking everyone in. We've been ordered not to go outside so everyone's at home."

"But I rang loads of people today and no-one was home!"

"And quite right too. We've been told to switch off all means of communication as they might draw the hole towards them. Apparently, it drifts along like snow and wherever there's some means of communication it swallows it right up."

"Just a sec," I said. I was beginning to get a handle on things. "You're talking about the collider, aren't you?"

"That's it."

"It's produced a black hole?"

"That's right, it's what they warned about earlier. Now it's growing at a rate of knots. No-one knows exactly how big it is now," said the stranger with a sigh. "I don't care. Let it suck them in. There's no-one in the world waiting for me. That's just how things turned out."

"And when did you last watch the news?"

"Yesterday. The TV's been off since this morning. That's what I'm saying, all communications are down. They said they'll keep us informed through loudspeakers."

"What if I turn the Internet on?"

"You can't. You can't do anything, don't you understand or what? I dare say that's been switched off as well. And the electricity's off – everywhere, all over the world."

"So they fixed the collider after all?"

"Must have done. Who knows?"

I was stupefied. The coils of my brain shifted as slowly as gears: there was no light, no Internet, no radio, no people. So what was there? Books, candles? Grabbing five packets of spaghetti in case of nuclear war, a pack of butter, and two dozen eggs, I went to the till. I turned round to say goodbye but already there was nobody there.

"And now my torch has failed as well. How are you meant to find a battery in the dark?" There was the stranger. I picked him out with the beam of my torch, found him some batteries, and got some to take home as well. We went to the till together. The Tajik woman said,

"The till's not working so pay what you like."

"What if I don't pay at all?" asked the stranger, brightening up.

"If you don't want to pay, don't," the woman virtually snarled.

I calculated the approximate value of my purchases and put down 500 roubles. I had the impression that money didn't mean anything anymore. Not for the Tajik woman, or for the shop, or for anyone at all.

"Goodbye," I said as I went out.

The stranger didn't reply and shuffled off in his own direction. Hunched over like a little old man.

I arrived back home with the food, opened the fridge, and found a puddle. Of course, there was no electricity! My butter was dissolving, like haze off apple trees. I checked the gas – at least that gas was working. I'd be able to stop the butter going off. I went upstairs to my neighbours. Naturally, the bell wasn't working. I knocked and knocked and eventually she opened the door. Her hair was sticking up all over the place. She was in her dressing gown. The flat was quiet. Indeed, quiet reigned over all. Perhaps that was why when she spoke it was in a whisper.

"Do you believe in the black hole?"

"I've only just been told about it. I'm completely out of touch."

"Then listen," she said. She sat me down in the kitchen and put the kettle on the stove. All three rings blazed in blue circles, probably, so that the only thing that could still be switched on, was. I also registered that for a long time I'd had only an electric kettle. I'd have to boil water in a pan.

"This the morning I turned the TV on. They were talking about the hole. I went straight onto the net and saw the headlines: a nuclear explosion, war. It took my breath away and then everything went blank. The TV went on working for a while, talking about the collider and saying there was a warning… I can't remember what about now. They're always telling us lies, more and more lies."

"And where's your husband?"

"Asleep. As soon as he heard, he chucked a bottle of vodka down his throat and that was that. Do you think they turned everything off on purpose? So that we wouldn't know what was really going on?"

"Very probably," I said, distractedly. For some reason, I really wanted to go home, lie on the sofa, light a candle, since it was already starting to go dark, and just lie there until something became clear by itself. Then again, I had an old telephone somewhere up in the attic. I could put that on. Someone might suddenly ring. The ordinary phone wasn't working.

I said a hasty goodbye to my neighbour and put my plan into action. I plugged in the rotary dial phone and tried it out. There was a dialling tone. I decided to ring Isa. I remembered that she also had a telephone from the last previous century at home. Isa answered.

"How are things with you, Isa?"

"I'm not well," she said, "I've really aged, like the world. I will pass away when it does. As for what's next, I don't understand. There aren't any people there. None at all.

Hang on in there for the moment. And just so you know, I'm Georgian," and she hung up.

Suddenly, the phone rang: a voice chirruped in the receiver, as distant as if it was coming from the Moon.

"Tanya, it's Rosa. Rosa, remember me?

"Of course, I do, Rosa. Where are you?"

"I don't know. I found a phone and it seems to be working. I wanted to say I'm sorry. It was Pushkin. It was!"

"Are you scared?" I asked.

"Yes," Rosa replied. "There are no people here."

"No, there aren't. There are no people," I concurred.

Glagoslav Publications Catalogue

- *The Time of Women* by Elena Chizhova
- *Sin* by Zakhar Prilepin
- *Hardly Ever Otherwise* by Maria Matios
- *The Lost Button* by Irene Rozdobudko
- *Khatyn* by Ales Adamovich
- *Christened with Crosses* by Eduard Kochergin
- *The Vital Needs of the Dead* by Igor Sakhnovsky
- *A Poet and Bin Laden* by Hamid Ismailov
- *Kobzar* by Taras Shevchenko
- *White Shanghai* by Elvira Baryakina
- *The Stone Bridge* by Alexander Terekhov
- *King Stakh's Wild Hunt* by Uladzimir Karatkevich
- *Depeche Mode* by Serhii Zhadan
- *Saraband Sarah's Band* by Larysa Denysenko
- *Herstories*, An Anthology of New Ukrainian Women Prose Writers
- *The Hawks of Peace* by Dmitry Rogozin
  by Leonid Andreev
- *The Battle of the Sexes Russian Style* by Nadezhda Ptushkina
- *A Book Without Photographs* by Sergey Shargunov
- *Sankya* by Zakhar Prilepin
- *Wolf Messing – The True Story of Russia's Greatest Psychic* by Tatiana Lungin
- *Good Stalin* by Victor Erofeyev
- *Solar Plexus* by Rustam Ibragimbekov
- *Don't Call me a Victim!* by Dina Yafasova
- *A History of Belarus* by Lubov Bazan
- *Children's Fashion of the Russian Empire* by Alexander Vasiliev
- *Empire of Corruption – The Russian National Pastime* by Vladimir Soloviev
- *Heroes of the 90s – People and Money. The Modern History of Russian Capitalism*
- *Boris Yeltsin – The Decade that Shook the World* by Boris Minaev
- *A Man Of Change – A study of the political life of Boris Yeltsin*
- *Gnedich* by Maria Rybakova
- *Marina Tsvetaeva – The Essential Poetry*

More coming soon…